Traps

Traps

MACKENZIE BEZOS

ALFRED A. KNOPF   NEW YORK   2013

THIS IS A BORZOI BOOK
PUBLISHED BY ALFRED A. KNOPF

All rights reserved. Published in the United States by
Alfred A. Knopf, a division of Random House, Inc., New York,
and in Canada by Random House of Canada Limited, Toronto.
www.aaknopf.com

Knopf, Borzoi Books, and the colophon are registered trademarks of
Random House, Inc.

Library of Congress Cataloging-in-Publication Data

Bezos, MacKenzie.
Traps / by MacKenzie Bezos.—1st ed.
p. cm.
"This is a Borzoi book."
ISBN 978-0-307-95973-7 (hardcover)
1. Self-realization in women—Fiction.   I. Title.
PS3602.E96T73 2013
813'.6—dc23   2012029032

Front-of-jacket photographs, left to right: Caroline von Tuempling /
Stockbyte / Getty Images; Dennis Hallinen / Getty Images; Richard Nowitz /
National Geographic / Getty Images; Pixtal / Superstock

Jacket design by Chip Kidd

Manufactured in the United States of America

First Edition

to my mother and father

Sweet are the uses of adversity,
Which, like the toad, ugly and venomous,
Wears yet a precious jewel in his head.

— SHAKESPEARE

Contents

Day 1

Day 2

Day 3

Day 4

Day 1

1

Nausea

In the vast valley north of Los Angeles, on a street of abandoned warehouses, behind a wall of corrugated metal topped with barbed wire, beyond an unused machine shop, in an unmarked prefab office building, inside a tiny bathroom with a hollow-core door, our first hero begins to tremble as she steps into a strange pair of pants.

These pants are enormous—inches thick, visibly stiff, made of a fabric coarse and gray—and when she grips the sink for balance, letting them fall, they relax only slightly, a pair of heavy phantom legs leaning against her own. A matching jacket lies felled on the floor like some hunted thing, arms pinned beneath its own weight. On the seat of the closed toilet, an open equipment bag bears a padded red helmet, its dark metal face cage regarding the water-stained ceiling. And on the floor beside it, a clipboard:

McClelland Security Services
Contingency Stress Inoculation Training
Dana Bowman, Years 1–6

with colored graph lines for Heart Rate and Test Duration descending.

This woman keeps her head bowed, focusing resolutely on the shining silver drain stop at the bottom of the sink. She is able to still herself this way, but over the course of a long minute, the short hair at the back of her neck begins to darken, the skin to shine, and at last a bead forms and slides down to disappear into the rolled cotton edge of her tank. She cranks the sink water on. She flips a wall switch, setting an old ceiling fan rattling. Finally she straightens and pulls the pants up tall, fitting her arms through the ragged straps of the suspenders in front of the mirror. Tall and lean. Short, dark hair. Eyes a clear green. Thin white line of a scar above her upper lip.

This is Dana.

She stops the stream of water with a still-shaking hand and cups some, sips at it, the bulk of it dribbling from her chin into the sink. She reaches behind her into the equipment bag to grab a long black strip of nylon webbing with a plastic clip. She passes it under the running tap and hikes her tank up to fit it on around her rib cage under her bra, weaving it through the suspender straps and snapping it in front over her sternum. Beyond the red helmet, in the deep of the bag, is a little black wristband with a digital display. She takes a deep breath through her nose—nothing you can hear, but you can see her chest rise and keep silently rising, followed by a long, slow fall. Then she fishes out the wristband: forty-four beats per minute.

She shuts the water off now and takes two neoprene sleeves from the bag and pulls them on over her forearms. She hefts the coat from the floor like you would a heavy backpack, slinging it on, tiny inside it, and makes short work of the clips in front. Then she picks up the clipboard, tucks the helmet under one arm, and opens the bathroom door.

On to a large break room. At the counter is a big young man in a T-shirt and camouflage cargo pants, his brown head shaved shiny bald. He is leaning against a humming microwave, tapping a spoon in his open palm. "Shit," he says. "The corsage I got isn't going to match."

Dana lumbers past him, setting her things on the table, and twists the dial on a padlock. Inside her locker is an oversized backpack—black ballistic nylon girded with a dozen zippered pockets. He watches as she yanks one open and withdraws a box of Pepto-Bismol tablets and fiddles with a crinkling cellophane sheet.

"Cujo-itis?" he says.

She pops a pair of pink tablets into her mouth and shuts her locker door. She twists the dial on the padlock again, and grabs the helmet and clipboard. The color is back in her face now, not so quickly from the pills, of course, but from some internal effort of her own. She manages to smile at him, even. "Smell of your mom's leftovers," she says, and she pushes the bar release on a fire door and steps, squinting, out into the bright courtyard.

Or not a courtyard, really. A half acre of sparkling mica-flecked blacktop hemmed in by those barb-topped walls and bulwarked by the unused warehouses beyond. To one side a line of six black SUVs with dark windows, windshields flashing white in the sun. At the far end a few long runs of chain-link fence leading to a low concrete outbuilding. And at the center a man in a tie and shirtsleeves next to a plain white service van. When the door crashes shut, the little building in the far corner of the yard explodes with muffled barking.

Dana lifts the helmet and swings open the face guard as she crosses the blacktop. She parts the flaps of thick foam at the neck and lowers it over her head, shutting the cage over her pale green eyes and the little white scar. It muffles her hearing, but right away (she will never understand this about herself, but she will continue to crave it) her heart rate slows and her focus sharpens. A paper clip on the blacktop. A helicopter banking south so far off in the turquoise sky she cannot hear it. And just before she reaches him, a flash of something at her examiner's neck as he reaches out for the clipboard. Someone (a barber? his wife?) has nicked him with the clippers just above his collar, a nearly invisible line of fine red marks just below the short hairs, like perforations. Corey Sifter is his name. A former Marine Aircraft Wing Commander and Combat Tactics Instructor from Alabama. Who likes the chair nearest the door in the break room and eats sunflower seeds in his office.

Dana hands him the clipboard and the wristband to her heart-rate monitor, and in turn he hands her a different wristband—no display, just a white plastic box with a single red button. She slips it on and pushes it up a bit, hiding it inside the sleeve of the big coat.

He says, "Now, you know that's not just a token of our affection. You can press that thing if you need us."

"Yes, sir."

"You were in there so long last year, we thought maybe you forgot. Decided you had no choice but to make a roommate out of him and live out your days in the back of that van."

"I like living alone, sir," she says.

He laughs. "Fair enough." He riffles the pages on the clipboard and then raps it with his knuckle. "I'm just hoping you don't fall asleep this time. Your peak heart rate has dropped by at least seven points every year."

Dana blinks inside her helmet, waiting. She knows such exchanges can go on a long time if she participates in them, and she is itching to get inside the van. She is still hot inside her suit; she is still nauseous. He still has the trace of a smile on his face people wear when they expect that their banter will be returned, but finally it falls away. He coughs and raps his knuckles again on his clipboard.

"All right then," he says.

And Dana opens the barn doors at the rear of the van and climbs in, pulling them shut behind her.

The space is dark after the bright outside, but it is also familiar. The pair of bucket seats scabbed with duct tape and the empty rear compartment stripped down to the white sheet-metal skin. An anarchy of scratch marks on the floor as her eyes adjust. The space does for her what the helmet did, and she kneels in the center of the van and feels carefully along the underside of the seats. She leans forward to click the glove box gently open and shut. She does not watch through the windshield as a door in the far building swings open. There is just the soft sifting of her hands along the floor beneath the dashboard, searching, and the rattle of her sneakers as she turns and steps back behind the bucket seats, while outside, silent beyond the van windows, a big German shepherd barrels out, dragging a handler by a leash. It scrabbles toward the van, and Dana crouches on one knee, extending her left arm just as the barn doors swing open, flooding the van with light, and the dog flies at her, teeth bared.

It is as she expects it to be. The van doors slam shut, plunging them into darkness, and the dog's jaws clamp down on the arm Dana feeds him. He has her just below the elbow, snarling and tugging, his claws scrabbling and slipping on the bare metal floor, and she pumps it in his mouth to keep him engaged as she waits for her eyes to adjust again and then scans: ceiling, spare tire well, door handles, window frames, tool kit. When she is sure she has covered it—the whole back half—she relaxes her arm knowing he will release it for a grip on something new, bored, and he does. As she turns to face forward, he lunges for her shoulder, his teeth knocking hard against the bone and throwing her into the back of the passenger seat, and as they fall together to the floor, Dana thinks her shoulder does hurt, she can feel that muffled somewhere deep below the surface of her attention, but it is precisely then that she detects what she has been searching for—the barest hint of it on the sunlit armrest of the front passenger door. The pivot lid on the ashtray is ajar. Its silver edge glints.

As she struggles to right herself, the dog grabs her by the back of her coat, trying to shake her whole body now, but Dana can just reach it, stretching her fingers out of the end of the tapered sleeve and flicking open the tiny metal lid. And this, right now, this moment is what Dana loves. She feels almost serene, seeing the key there in the ashtray and knowing just how she will grab it, just how she will pull it back into her fist and then into the sleeve of her armor, just how she will crouch before she explodes upward to throw the dog back into the closed barn doors. He doesn't let go of her jacket when she does it, but it doesn't matter. When she ends up on her back on the van floor, for the tenth of a second it takes him to right himself and land with his front paws on her chest, Dana does absolutely nothing. She waits for him to come, his teeth clattering against her face guard, wild, glistening, enormous, a child's nightmare. It should be terrifying, but she has the key tight in her right hand and she is working a boot up under his belly, and Dana shoves, catapulting him against the spare tire. It gives her all the time she needs to roll onto one knee and dive for the steering column. As he lands on her back and bites down on the fabric at her neck, he crushes her against the parking brake, and her helmet bounces on the bucket seat, but she can just reach now, and on her second fumble she slides the key into the ignition. She turns it and the engine rumbles on, and at the sound of it, like magic—like something from a cartoon, really—the dog lets go of her jacket and lies down on the floor of the van, as if ready for a nap, or a pat.

As soon as Dana's examiner opens the doors, the nausea returns. She hops out and takes off past him at a trot. She types a code into a keypad next to the building door and pulls it open, rushing past the big young man eating soup from a bowl at the table and into the tiny bathroom, shutting the door on our view of her.

We are out in the break room, where the big young man has paused over his bowl of soup and the examiner is just stepping in through the fire door, clipboard in hand. Velasquez is another of the firm's agents—he has worked protective shifts with Dana a hundred times—and Corey Sifter coached her through a high-speed-emergency driving course and an evacuation simulation in a smoke- and flame-filled room, but neither man has ever been shown a photo on her BlackBerry or heard her describe a movie she saw over a weekend or watched her drink a beer. Through the hollow-core door to the bathroom now comes the clear sound of retching and coughing. Velasquez looks down at his food, and Corey Sifter at the statistics before him. They steal glances at the door as the sounds from within change. A toilet flushing. The rattle of a paper-towel dispenser. Running water. And finally the door clicks open and Dana emerges, her face dry and pale and her hair glistening with sweat or sink water, in her damp tank top and running shorts, the heavy bite suit draped over one arm and the helmet under the other.

She heaps them onto the break table next to the empty equipment bag and peers down at Corey Sifter's clipboard.

"How'd I do?" she says to him.

He coughs. He looks at her wristband and then back at the clipboard. "Five beats down on pulse and about a minute faster than your best speed."

Even as he speaks she is stepping around him to her locker, and he turns, watching her. He runs a hand through his buzz cut.

She unzips the top of her backpack and takes out a hooded sweatshirt and pulls it on over the tank she fought in.

"Where you headed?" he says.

"Home."

"What's your hurry? How about you stop by Shannon's office before you go? Let her check your vitals."

"I don't think that's necessary."

"Just heart rate and blood pressure. She'll have you out in five."

"I appreciate your concern, sir—"

"Corey, Dana. We've been working together for seven years."

"I appreciate it, I do. But I don't think it's necessary."

"Sometimes the heat gets to people in there—"

"It wasn't that, sir—Corey."

"Or the adrenaline buildup." He picks up the receiver on the break-room phone. "She'll check you out real fast."

Dana shoulders her backpack and shuts her locker, leaving it empty. "I was queasy before I tested. Velasquez saw me take something for it before I came out."

Corey Sifter looks at Velasquez in his place at the table.

The big young man nods, gesturing with his spoon, his mouth full. He swallows. "True story."

"Something I ate, maybe," Dana says.

He sets down the phone. "I'll have to note it in your file."

"Of course."

He shakes his head. "And you'll have to be sure to report it in the Protective Asset Inventory on your next duty check-in."

"Certainly," Dana says, turning.

"And, Dana?"

She turns back to him.

"We like a pilot who can fly without a wingman. We do. But not if she won't keep her radio on."

Outside she steps through a small corrugated metal door in a corrugated metal wall into a street of locked-up warehouses and garbage-choked gutters. Down at the corner a few men sit on the curb outside a taqueria, but other than that the street is empty. Just a lunch bag blowing, and a few parked cars, including Dana's white Jetta, and a big black crow sitting on her roof. He could almost be looking at her, she thinks, and in fact, as she gets closer, she sees that he is. He cocks his head, his black eyes staring, and only when she takes out her key to open the door does he fly away, wheeling up and off over another razor-wire fence to a place she can't see and never will. She gets in her car, locks her door, and sets her big backpack on the seat beside her. Behind her, hanging down from the hook and bending at the waist against the seat like a passenger, is a white cotton dress with peach-colored flowers still in the clear bag from a department store.

The drive out of that valley into Los Angeles is long. And silent for Dana. She does not turn the radio on. She watches the road. And at stoplights her eyes catch on the out-of-place and the furtive: a woman sitting on a suitcase; a boy opening a bag in a dark doorway; a man in a parked car outside the high-fenced play yard of a school. She passes from the narrow streets of those closed-up blocks, to the stoplighted boulevard of the flat valley, up onto a highway that bears her between brown hills until she can see the beach and ocean, and then off and down to more stoplighted streets that draw her into her own neighborhood, Culver City, with its streets of single-story houses just big enough for an arched front door and two flanking windows, well kept every one. Neat streets. With clean gutters and sidewalks and tiny squares of clipped lawn, and then a tidy little alley alongside her own street's one apartment building, white and U-shaped around a courtyard of vinyl-strap lawn furniture, with windows overlooking, all of them closed, save for three at the top with scraps of curtain each cut from a different patterned bedsheet, billowing out in the breeze like flags. Dana pulls into the little alley and through a garage door and down into the low-ceilinged parking area underneath.

Dark and cool and low, the garage is mostly full at this hour, but she finds a slim space. Her shoes make a gritty sound in the echoey dim as she crosses, beetle-backed in her big backpack and carrying the dress high to keep it from dragging. It trails behind her a bit at the hem, like a ghost. They ride up in the elevator together and emerge into the third-floor hallway, brown doors receding into the distance like beads on a string, and she stops in front of number three-twenty-four.

It is dim inside, all the louvered blinds drawn flush to the windowsills against the late afternoon sun, and Dana flicks on the lights to reveal an expanse of white wall-to-wall carpeting broken only by a white couch, a glass-topped coffee table, and a computer desk with a closed laptop. On the wall to the left of the couch, a bicycle hangs from a pair of hooks. Above the desk is an Escher print of infinite stairs. The silence inside this room is thick, almost cottony.

She shuts the door.

On the clean floor of the hall closet, beside two pairs of neatly aligned running shoes, there is a space for her backpack. Above it she hangs the peach-flowered dress. The bedroom beyond has a light blue blanket and a smooth fold of white topsheet beneath another Escher print—this one of triangle tiles that row by row part and change just slightly, until at the top they fly away as birds. She showers in a small clean bathroom where all the personal items hide secreted behind a mirror, and dresses in jeans and a white T-shirt and afterward steps to her living room window, where, with a slow pull of a cord, she draws the blinds half open, filling the white room with light. She cracks the window, and flamenco music drifts to her from across the way.

Then her phone rings.

Dana looks through the half-lowered eyelid of her metal blinds at the curtains luffing out across the way. On the windowsill, a green plant growing from the skull of a cow. She picks up the phone.

That same music and a man's voice: "You're home! I'm on the other line with my mom! Save me!"

Then a click and a dial tone.

Dana smiles. Although this trip is just down the hall, she puts on her sneakers. She slings her backpack over her shoulder. She locks her door behind her. She walks down the long gray carpet. Beige walls with brown doors. A welcome mat. A wreath of hay and dried flowers. A right-angle turn to the right, and more doors, and another right turn, and then the sound of Latin music draws her to a door where a pair of muddy sneakers lies untied and discarded, toes pointing in opposite directions on the threshold of a door that is half open.

When she pushes it wide, she is face-to-face with a red macaw on an open perch plucking a grape from a bowl of sliced bananas and oranges. Birdseed is scattered everywhere on the little square of white linoleum that marks the vestibule, and in the tangle of sneakers and boots and sandals below, cracked peanut shells and little pellets of millet line the insoles and fill the crossed laces.

The room beyond is similar in shape to her own, but larger. The white rug is covered with a big raggedly cut rectangle of bright green Astroturf, and the couch, on which a second parrot (blue and gold) sits preening, is draped with a Spider-Man bedsheet. In the corner a huge wooden Buddha sits cross-legged and delighted next to a terrarium criss-crossed with branches and bejeweled with tiny frogs. A sudden breeze pushes the curtains into the room like streamers and knocks the cow skull full of soil and green tendrils onto the floor. Standing in the kitchen in swim trunks and a yellow T-shirt, holding a cordless phone to his ear, the man who summoned her here does not notice this, though. He only notices her. His eyes widen at the sight of her standing behind his parrot. This is Ian.

"Mom, I have to go! I'll see you tomorrow, Dana's here!"

He turns on the water and tries to rinse his hand. "Yes, I'm bringing her with me this time so you can finally meet her." He wipes his dripping hand on the seat of his shorts, leaving a trace of green. "She's a volunteer EMT, I said, remember? I saw her in her uniform, and I asked her to teach me to do my Sylatron injections. . . ." He is rolling his eyes now and grinning. "Her regular job is in security services, yes. . . . Yes, it's crazy and appalling that you have to ask after we've been dating almost a year. . . ." He raises his eyebrows and runs a hand through his messy blond hair. "Yes, we plan to continue living in sin for a while. . . . No, actually that's a common misconception, sin only gets better with age. . . ." He winks at Dana. "Tomorrow, yes, and I have a perfectly good suit, yes. I know that weddings start at a specific time, yes. And in this case it's seven o'clock in San Marino, yes. I love you, yes. Okay, gotta go."

When he hangs up, his hands shoot into the air. He takes two big strides, cradles her head between his hands, stamps a kiss on her mouth, and pulls back grinning. Then he fingers her backpack straps and pulls them off—one, two—eyeing her slyly, as if they were straps on lingerie.

"Hi," she says, and her eyes flit (she can't help it) to the ridge of scar tissue in a patch of reddened skin just below his left ear.

"Any oozing?" he says.

"No." She shakes her head and squeezes her eyes shut a second. "Sorry." She opens her eyes. "What are you making over there?"

"I was at the Venice Market, and there was this beautiful Puerto Rican woman with ice blue eyes and six little kids running around and two Colt 45 cartons, one full of Rottweiler puppies and the other full of ripe avocados marked 'Whole box, fifteen dollars.' I figured you'd be happy I came home with the avocados."

"Instead of the Puerto Rican woman?"

He laughs (gigantic; explosive; a joyous gunshot) and says, "Instead of one of the puppies, I meant."

"A puppy I wouldn't have minded."

"Aha! 'Minded,' though! That's the key word. I don't want anything to jeopardize my slow and steady, make-moving-in-with-Ian-easy-and-attractive plan."

She eyes the birds and the frogs. "I don't think a puppy would have tipped the scales much."

"Is that a yes?" He grins, and before she can answer he grabs her by the back of the neck and plants another kiss on her forehead. "So I tweeted about the avocados, and now I might have as many as four hundred and eighty-nine people showing up in an hour for guacamole and this drink I found on the Internet that's blue, and I need you to taste everything because I still can't taste."

"What's in the drink?"

"Rum and blue Kool-Aid mostly, with green sugar on the rim. I just wanted it to be blue and green, like the Sylatron box. Here, taste the guacamole, would you?"

He has mashed it in a large frying pan with a scuffed black plastic handle. He dips a finger in and offers it to her and she takes a tentative lick. She squeezes her eyes shut again, smiling and wincing at the same time. "*So salty!*"

"See! That's what I need you for! Or one thing, anyway. I was seasoning it while I was talking to my mom and I got distracted. Help me add more avocados."

Dana washes her hands at the sink, soaping them so thoroughly it makes him grin. She holds her dripping hands upturned like a surgeon, looking around his counter at the crumpled hand towels, the box of hypodermic needles, and the pile of mail, and finally takes a paper napkin from a plastic bag lolling in the mash of green.

He says, "Hey, how's your nausea?"

"Thriving."

"Have you thought about seeing a doctor? Maybe it's not the triathlon training. Maybe you've got some kind of bug. Swine flu. West Nile. Encephalitis."

"I'm pretty sure it's the training."

"Maybe it's sympathy nausea! 'Radiation Side Effects Particularly Strong in Devoted Lovers of Melanoma Patients, New Study Reveals.' "

"It's worse after exertion, mostly after the longer runs."

"Or hey! When was the last time you got your period?"

"A girl like me does *not* get inadvertently pregnant, Ian."

"Accidents happen—"

"Only to disorganized people."

"There's always room for serendipity."

"I take the pill, *and* I make you use a condom."

"Okay, fair point. I have some ginger ale in the fridge if you want some."

"That sounds pretty good, actually."

She opens the refrigerator. Inside is a loaf of white bread, a six-pack of ginger ale, and one can of Boost nutritional supplement drink. She pulls out a ginger ale and cracks it open and takes a sip.

Then she goes to her backpack and brushes aside the millet and bits of peanut shell and opens a zippered compartment to withdraw a little plastic tube of multivitamin tablets—the kind you drop into water and make fizz. Ian is watching her. She takes a glass from his cupboard and drops an orange disk in the bottom with a tinkling sound. She fills it up with water and slides it toward him among the dark skins.

He watches it dissolve, hissing. An ugly lacing of yellow foam rims the top of the glass.

"It's good for you," she says.

"Maybe."

"It can't hurt."

"We'll see."

"Humor me?"

He smiles at her. "As long as we both shall live," and he gulps it down, tipping his head back, the ridge of scar exposed. Dana looks away, her eyes settling on his messy counter: the plastic bag of paper napkins, his keys and wallet, the sea of skins and streaks of avocado and a box of needles not quite closed and that pile of mail, slipping among the pits and peels. A postcard. A utility bill. An ad for a wireless plan. An open envelope from Aetna insurance, the top of it sticking out with a phone number handwritten in purple crayon across the top:

Dear Mr. Freeman:
We regret to inform you . . .

"What's that from Aetna?" she says.

"Just a letter."

"What do they regret to inform you?"

"They denied one of my claims." He takes another avocado and slices it open with a heedless little zip of his paring knife.

"For how much?"

"Thirty thousand-ish."

"That's terrible!"

"We'll see."

"How can you say that?"

He squeezes the yellow-green into the pan. "I'm sure it will all work out in the end."

"How?"

"One thing will happen. And then another and another. And so on."

She grabs the letter. At the top is an incongruous blue-and-yellow logo—a stick figure with arms upraised to catch rays of light. Dana goes to her backpack and takes out a pen and a tiny notebook. "Do you mind if I write some of this down?"

"Not if you don't mind my finding your relentless notetaking mysteriously arousing."

She crouches among the seeds and writes, "Sylatron. . . . 888 micrograms. . . . Aetna Claims Division."

Ian is wiping his hands on his shorts as he moves to crouch next to her. He has to stand under the bird perch to do it, and he settles in beside her, the millet and hulls cracking beneath his bare feet. He kisses her on the shoulder.

"Hold on a sec," she says, and keeps scribbling.

He kisses her again. "I can appeal it, Dana. It happens all the time with cancer treatments."

"Can I borrow this for a night? There's so much here."

"You can borrow anything," he says.

She makes another note. Then closes her notebook and slips it in a little pocket with the letter, folding it small.

He says, "What else have you got in there?"

She smiles and zips the pocket shut.

He says, "Please? Just a few things?"

She rolls her eyes, but she unzips the top compartment and reaches inside. She draws out a roll of duct tape. A ziplock bag of zip ties. A ziplock bag of ziplock bags.

"Temptress," he says.

She pulls out a set of tiny screwdrivers. A box of matches. A pair of black sandals. A small white-noise machine and a little box of earplugs.

"Vixen."

She laughs then and turns awkwardly to kiss him, a long kiss, both of them squatting over her backpack under the bird stand among his dirty shoes.

He says, "Will you stay for the party?"

She winces.

"Is that a yes?"

She puts the duct tape back in the bag. "I have twenty-three steps in my latest sleep-improvement regime." She puts away the matches and the zip ties.

He says, "Maybe that's part of the problem."

"What is?"

"All the steps. A regime."

She gathers the remaining things and arranges and rearranges them inside. He himself falls asleep so easily. She has seen it many times before she steals back to her snow white room, his arms and legs splayed wide in the center of his churned sheets, his lips parted. Sometimes tiny tears form at the outer corners of his closed blue eyes.

He says, "Maybe what you need is a super late night of blue drinks and the comfort of sleeping in an unfamiliar bed with a charming snorer who adores you."

She is still shifting things around in her bag. "It's just the way I'm built, Ian. That should comfort me—I'm with you on that—but it doesn't. You know what comforts me?" She takes her hand out of her backpack and looks at him squarely.

"Tell me."

"Being alone. Being in my own room alone. Or even—it's crazy, get this—wearing a costume. Helmets too. Helmets comfort me. And sinking to the bottom of a public pool. Or here's another weird one—being in a motel room. An empty, sterile, anonymous motel room."

"You sleep well in motel rooms?"

"Well, no. But I feel comfortable in them. They soothe me."

She takes the duct tape out one last time and moves it to the other side. The two of them are crouched so close together their faces are almost touching. Her elbow grazes him as she jockeys things around.

He says, "I love this backpack, Dana. This backpack has appeared in all five of my favorite dreams. But I'm telling you, whatever finally helps you sleep peacefully, it isn't going to be in this backpack."

"Why?" she says with mock surprise. "What's missing?"

"They don't make ziplocks for everything."

"You do know they come in gallon and snack size now, right?"

"Some things can't be bagged."

"Like what?"

"Luck."

"You're so superstitious."

"It's not superstition. It's respect for the inexplicable, and actually you've got plenty."

"Name one example."

"All those things you try to help you sleep. What is that if not voo-doo?"

Everything is back in her backpack now, and she zips the top shut.

"I'm sorry," she says. She looks tired, but Ian is smiling, and his eyes are soft on her.

She says, "You're probably right. But for tonight at least, I better stick with my twenty-three steps. I want to be well rested for work and your sister's wedding tomorrow. I know how important it is to you."

He shrugs, still smiling. "We'll see."

"Besides"—she stands up, hefting the pack—"you've given me a project. You know how I like a project."

The intercom rings then, and she turns and puts her hand on the doorknob, but he rises quickly and lays a hand against the door to stop her opening it. He presses the button on the intercom. "Avocasa!" he says. "Enter to be delighted!" Then he releases the button and lays his hand on Dana's shoulder. Pieces of birdseed drop from their clothes to the floor, a soft ticking like the end of a rain.

"Dana," he says. "I know it's not the birds. Or the frogs. Or your insomnia."

She keeps her chin level, but she cuts her eyes away to a point just beyond his face. She says, "I just think we should wait a while."

"I know uncertainty is not your best thing, but the truth is, anything can happen. The treatment could work and I could live to be a hundred, still teaching surfing and annoying my neighbors with flamenco music. I could get hit by a bus tomorrow on my way to Rite Aid to buy more Boost."

"Not if I buy you more Boost."

He closes his eyes and presses a last kiss on her forehead. They can hear footsteps approaching in the hall. He takes his hand off the door.

"Have fun tonight," she says, and then she steps out into the long beige hallway and turns left, away from his guests, and walks away without looking back. The sound of his Spanish music shimmies and pumps behind her and fades a bit each time she turns the corner, turns the corner, past the dark brown doors and the one little welcome mat, one little wreath, past her own door to the elevator to the garage.

The Boost, it turns out, is at the end of an aisle stocked disconcertingly with bedpans and adult diapers, and it takes her a second, standing there in the fluorescent light, to make herself move to take some from the shelf. The Muzak from above is something familiar but slowed down, and played with a tinny-sounding piano that makes her sad. The cans are grouped in packs of twelve, slipcovered in a cardboard case with a handle at the top, and when she places her hands on a pair at eye level on the top shelf and slides them back and off, taking their weight like a village girl with two buckets of water, she sees that there, pressed against the white perforated metal back wall of the shelving where the two cases of Boost used to be, is a single boxed pregnancy test.

Dana looks up and down the aisle for other boxes like it, but of course there are none. It is an aisle for the sick and dying. The box is pink, with a picture of a delighted woman holding the white plastic test stick, and a band of blue reads, "Second Test Free Inside." On the shelf on either side of it is a thin furry strip of dust, where the cases of Boost never reach.

Back in the garage she finds the door to Ian's green Volkswagen unlocked, as she knew she would, and she places the cases of Boost on his seat. Her apartment is dark now, but her window is still cracked and through it she can hear the flamenco music and the laughter from his party. She passes through her dark living room and flicks on the lights in her bathroom, and from her backpack she withdraws the boxed test. The instruction sheet crackles as she takes it out. She examines the pictograms. She reads the tiny print. She pulls down her pants and holds the stick between her legs, staring at her socks on the floor on the blue circle of rug. A faint chorus of cheers floats in from Ian's party, and she recaps the stick and sets it facedown on the counter and fastens her pants and then flushes and washes her hands, soaping thoroughly. When she has dried them, she flips it over and sees that she is in fact pregnant.

Over the next hour, even with the blinds drawn and the window closed fully, she can hear the backbeat from Ian's music. The Planned Parenthood website shows eight clinics offering abortion services within a ten-mile radius of her apartment. The American Cancer Society recommends a fifteen-step process for handling a denial of claim for prescribed treatments. The Patient Advocate Foundation has several sample letters of appeal. She owes him the news, she knows this, but it is ten o'clock, and his apartment is full of people, and the news is not only private, but also (she is certain) to him it will be heartbreakingly sad. Dana's printer whirs and clicks, and she collates and staples as the papers roll out into the tray. She labels folders. She separates her printouts inside them with little colored tabs. Last, from under her keyboard she takes a cream-colored envelope addressed to Ms. Dana Bowman. There is an invitation inside it to the wedding, and a little card with printed directions to the chapel in San Marino where she will meet Ian after work. She will tell him in the parking lot in case he does not want her to stay. She adds this to the stack, and fits all of it neatly into a large flat pocket at the back of her backpack.

Then Dana irons her dress, setting up the board and iron in the center of her living room and doing a good job, taking care at the seams not to make the cloth pucker, and she zips it back into the clear bag and hangs it again in her closet.

When she slips into bed she is wearing just plain cotton underpants and a long white T-shirt. A black sleep mask and a pair of earplugs lie on the nightstand at the base of the lamp. She twists a switch to lower the light to a cavelike dimness, and she presses a button on her iPod, and the man's voice is so soft and gentle it is almost shaky. There are long pauses, a minute or more, between the things he says.

"First, lie on your back with your arms and legs at a distance from each other that allows you to relax them completely. . . ."

"Notice if you are holding any tension anywhere else in your body. . . ."

"Notice your jaw. . . ."

"Notice your tongue. . . ."

During the pauses there is only her breathing, and the distracting bass thumping from Ian's party, but lying there in the orderly dim, centered on the big bed beneath the print of triangle tiles that waver and change into birds, Dana ignores the backbeat and follows her plan.

2

Old Dogs

S ix miles from Dana's apartment, a second woman stands shoulder to shoulder with her husband at the kitchen sink, setting down a bread plate for him to wash. He reaches around to press a hand to the side of her head and pull her in and kiss her above the ear, on her dark golden hair. Then she walks to the table to get more. Cut strawberries and a wooden bowl of salad and the last of the salmon steaks he'd made. Two mugs of milk half empty. Two glasses of wine. Their kitchen is big—with a butcher-block island and a clay pizza oven—but so clotted with clutter it does not seem so. On the windowsill an avocado pit balances over a coffee mug next to a wilting Chia pet in the shape of Shrek's head. On the floor three hairy dog beds and stainless-steel water bowls flank a milk crate of wheels and popsicle sticks and doll arms marked "Broken Things." On a wall of shelves, picture books have been crammed in at every odd angle, and a clear bin of toys bears a stuffed elephant, a Mrs. Potato Head, and an Oscar statuette in a Barbie dress. And here on the counter, lying still and small and seemingly harmless among the dirty dinner plates and the unfinished homework assignments and the baskets of dog medication and overripe fruit, is a cell phone this woman looks at each time she passes to and from the sink. When she has cleared the whole table—when she is passing back with a yellow sponge to work at the drips of ketchup and coins of carrot on the vinyl bench cushion—it rings.

Her husband looks at her. She is kneeling on the bench, not looking up from her work, a beautiful woman in a bulky sweatshirt and thread-bare man's slippers with a face contorted by sorrow and tension. This is Jessica. She lets the phone ring, and he steps to the counter and glances at the number flashing in the display—a number with a 702 area code. She is pinching up the carrot pieces with her fingers, and when she backs off the bench, he sees that her eyes are welling.

He says, "Don't forget why you're doing it."

It stops then, and she crosses to dump the carrot pieces in the sink. He kisses her again on the hair just as two dark-haired girls enter the kitchen in matching pajamas. The younger one wears a pair of sparkly red party shoes, and she has a stuffed dog tucked under her arm. Each of her steps leaves behind a ghost of glitter on the Mexican tile.

Jessica wipes under her eyes with thumb and forefinger before she turns to them.

"Guess what I have for dessert—s'mores!"

"The puffy kind?"

"Yes!"

"Lucky ducks," the husband says.

He is a fit Indian man in striped pajama pants and a T-shirt that says UCLA, and although he grew up in Orange County, an agnostic ER doctor who would have been content with a courthouse wedding, she had wanted to marry him in Mumbai in front of his enormous family. She had wanted him to arrive on horseback and walk with her seven times around a circle of fire. She had wanted to stand at the threshold to his mother's home and dip her feet in a paste of red powder and milk before stepping inside. He keeps working on the dishes, rinsing and setting them into the open dishwasher while she takes out the marshmallows and graham crackers and chocolate and sets them on the kitchen table next to two white china saucers haloed with tiny yellow flowers.

The older girl opens the box of graham crackers and draws out the waxed-paper sleeve. The smaller girl sets her dog on the table and they each stack a marshmallow on top of a cracker, and then the older girl makes a minute, unnecessary adjustment to her sister's work before placing the plates in the microwave and closing the door. They watch through the window, their heads pressed together and silhouetted against the light as the table inside turns, and Jessica watches them, and her husband watches her watching. He is the seventh of eight children, self-reliant, unruffled by drama, comfortable on the sidelines, accustomed to sharing. Until he met Jessica it did not occur to him that he might find in romance the deep fulfillment he found in his work in the pediatric ER, where with his friendly unassuming ease and decisive competence he could perform countless acts of salvation without fanfare or domination. A big family, self-acceptance, emotional simplicity, anonymity, a sense of humor, an upbringing in an ethnoculture of forgiveness—Akhil is stinking rich, a tree hung to bough-breaking weight with fruit Jessica starves for, while she herself, without intention or awareness, is the gigantic megawatt center of their family universe. Her purposeful photo collages, her ever-lengthening roster of arduously observed traditions, her midnight vigils of idealistic worries and questions—every day he forgets afresh how dim his own heart can grow until she lights it up again with her industrious, furrowed-brow ruminations. The girls feel it too, leaning toward her when her voice takes on that earnest tone retelling their little family stories, webbing their lives with nostalgia and meaning. She makes everything beautiful. If Akhil is her hero, Jessica is the closest he has to any religion—a savior to him just the same. Watching her now he knows without asking that she is worried to the point of sweating that the phone will ring again with the girls in the room; behind her is a corkboard wall covered floor to ceiling with family photos (all his) that she has arranged in the shape of a tree.

"They're puffing!" the smaller girl says.

Jessica opens the microwave door and carries their plates back to the table, the marshmallows as big as baseballs now, high and wobbling.

Both girls know what to do. They grab squares of chocolate and second crackers to set on top, pressing, watching the big marshmallows spread and fall. Then they stand at the table eating, the melted marshmallows sliding and sticking whitely to their lips and the corners of their mouths, while behind them their mother resumes cleaning. Their father is putting away what they have not eaten, wrapping it in plastic, while Jessica wipes around the little white plates and the stuffed dog on the table with a sponge.

The cell phone rings again.

The girls see their father look at their mother, but she keeps wiping.

The older girl says, "Mom. Your phone."

"It's a wrong number," Jessica says.

The little girl says, "Why don't you answer, Mommy?"

"Because it's a wrong number," their father says. He refills their mother's wineglass. The phone keeps ringing.

"But they've been calling all day," the older girl says. "If she just answers, she could tell them."

"They'll figure it out," he says.

"How? She doesn't even have voice mail."

"They'll give up eventually."

"Somebody should tell them." She licks her fingers briskly. "I'll do it," she says, and as she takes a step toward the counter, Jessica turns from the sink and snatches up the phone in her damp hand.

It stops ringing.

"See there," their father says.

"They'll just try again," the big girl says.

He claps his hands together. "Who's for a movie?"

The older girl says, "Okay, but I'm holding the remote this time."

The little girl gives her a pleading look, but the big girl stands firm. "You did it last time and all we watched was the Munchkins over and over."

She clutches her dog to her chest. "The witch is scary, though!"

"You can tell me to pause if you want, but I'm sick of that stupid Lollipop Guild."

They stuff the last bites in their mouths and run off.

Jessica puts the phone in her sweatshirt pocket and takes a sip of her wine, her hand shaking.

From down the hall comes the sound of Judy Garland singing.

She says, "I'm not sure I can do this."

"What do you mean?"

"It feels terrible, Akhil. It feels like someone else's life."

"You didn't pick this; he did. Some things we don't get to pick."

She sips her wine again, her lashes damp.

He gestures with his head toward the desk in the corner. A two-foot stack sits next to the computer—a mix of padded mailers and loose stacks of white paper bound with brads. "Are any of them good?"

She shrugs.

"Have you read any?"

"A few."

He makes a quick circle with his glass on the counter and then watches the wine swirl and settle. For all his enjoyment of work in trauma, he draws his real satisfaction from his ability to help and to heal. And there is no escaping the diagnosis here. His wife is stuck. That when he met her she had a job she truly loved and under his care she has lost it and not found her way back sometimes chafes at him. It is beginning to seem to him that triage all those years ago in the months after her Oscar may have called for goading instead of patience.

"Jessica, tell me something. Just when do you think you'll get back in the water?"

"Soon."

"I know you miss it."

"It's nice to have all this time with the girls."

"You could have both, though. I could help."

"It's only been a little while."

"Four years, isn't it? And all of them holed up and hiding?"

"I am not hiding! I'm more social than you are! I'm with people all the time! Diwali and Holi with your family, and Prisha's Brownie camp-out, and the Pets with Disabilities fund-raiser, and Jaya's end-of-season soccer party, and my Buddhist book club and yoga retreats."

"You hosted all of that here."

"So? I'm sharing what we have! I'm making this a place the girls can be proud of. A beautiful shared community with a huge homemade extended family."

He slips her hand in his. "Jessica. I'm on your team. The life you're building here is beautiful. I love it. I'm lucky to be part of it. I'm just saying I think there might be some things you're avoiding."

"I'm not avoiding acting; I'm just taking a break."

"I didn't mean the acting," he says.

The day she met him she had been rushing out of a Starbucks in Santa Monica. She had tripped on a tree root jogging in a baggy sweat-suit, hat, and dark glasses. A voice behind her on the sidewalk said, "You've got toilet paper stuck to your sneaker." She stooped to remove it. ". . . and you're bleeding," the voice added. And when she straightened: "Uh-oh—also famous." He was wearing scrubs and an ID badge with a background of teddy bears. "Famous and aggressively and insufficiently camouflaged." He took a bandaid from his pocket and held it out to her. When she didn't take it, he smiled. "That's all I've got; the cut and the toilet paper are the only ones I can help with. My other pocket is just full of Elmo stickers."

Everything she loved about him was in that. She had married him for that moment.

Now when she says, "You agree with me then. You think I should answer it. You think I should talk to him," Akhil says, "God, no. I think you should change your cell phone number but stop letting the things they print in the tabloids keep you from leaving the house."

She turns to the wall of pictures by the door. The girls at gymnastics with Akhil's mother. At the playground with Akhil's sister. Reading books with Akhil's father. Playing gilli-danda in the street with Akhil's nieces and nephews on the annual visits they make to Mumbai. Twice a week he plays racquetball with an older brother who slept with his high school girlfriend. Every time they get together his father suggests that Akhil go back and do a residency toward a more prestigious specialty, and still Akhil calls him up once a week to meet him for coffee.

She says, "You would never do this."

"Yes I would."

" 'Life's too short for grudges,' you always say. 'Forgiveness takes less energy,' you always say. 'Family members are no uglier than other people, it's just that the lights in family rooms are so bright.' "

"All true, but beside the point in this case."

"Oh, bullshit. Face it. You would never in a million years stop talking to your family."

"But I won that lottery! My family is sane! I have no sociopaths or emotional blackmail artists in my family!"

"I don't want to be this kind of person, Akhil."

"Didn't he say something like that in one of his letters?"

"This is not what I want the girls to grow up with."

"That's exactly what he said in one of his letters!"

She changes her voice, high and innocent: "I thought Mommy didn't have a daddy," and "How come we only have one grandpa?" and then low and stagy: "Estrangement More Popular than Kabbalah with Hollywood's A-listers. Next on *Inside Edition.*"

The phone rings again in her pocket.

She takes it out and lays it on the counter for both of them to see: that same number.

For a few seconds they both stare at it together there on the counter. It slides and rotates slightly as it rings.

Finally she picks it up and presses a button.

"Hello?" she says.

"Jessica Lessing?" It is an elderly woman's voice. Jessica can hear a dog barking in the background.

"Yes?"

"My name is Eleanor Babbage. I'm the landlady for the unit in Summerlin you cosigned."

"Excuse me?"

"Outside Las Vegas? The house at Thirty-six Forty Villa Ridge? Rented to Gabriel Fletcher?"

"Oh." Her face pales. "I'm afraid there must be some mistake."

The barks of the dog are faint but consistent, almost like a metronome.

"But I've got your signature right here. You signed it in lovely purple ink and wrote this phone number right next to it."

"I'm afraid that's not my signature."

"Oh, no, dear. He showed me pictures. Pictures of him next to you with your baby girls in pajamas at Christmastime."

"Yes, yes. He is my father. It's just . . . " Jessica rubs her forehead. Akhil watches her from across the counter. She says, "Is that what this is about? The rental obligation?"

"What? Oh no—he's my favorite tenant. He even sent me flowers the day after I showed him the house! He was even willing to take a unit whose yard was still being landscaped! And the last month's rent and the damage deposit are completely covered by my share of his stake in your next film."

"What film?"

"He showed me the preproduction notes on the Internet. The costume sketches are divine. Is it the same girl who did the costumes for your Elizabeth and Mary movie? He wouldn't tell me. He said he didn't want to oversell it, but I guessed!"

Jessica rubs her forehead again. She clears her throat. Down the hall the music has the dizzy sound of the tracks they play when cartoon animals discover they are falling. In the background on the landlady's end of the line, the dog is still barking. She says, "Well then, um. . . . What seems to be the problem?"

"Oh yes. It's just that the neighbors have been complaining about his poor dog."

"His dog?"

"Yes. Grace Kelly has been out in the yard barking ever since he went to the hospital."

"Hospital?"

"Yes. You don't know? Oh for heaven's sake, this makes much more sense now, you always seem like such a lovely person in your films. I was in Palm Springs visiting my sister, and when I got back I resumed my usual weekly property visits, and this time, when I came around, your father's handsome white malamute was just barking in the backyard, and Mrs. Lippincott from next door comes rushing out into her driveway. Says an ambulance came to take him to the hospital shortly after I left town and the dog's been outside ever since. I say, 'Hospital?! Why, that's Jessica Lessing's father, you know. Have the papers reported a visit to town from her?' No, she says, not hardly. She herself has been dropping food over the fence each day just to keep the poor dog from starving. I say, 'That can't be. She would never let that happen. Remember her in *Personal History*? Remember her in *A Passage to the Heart*? I'm going to call her the instant I get back to my house.'"

Jessica rubs her temples. Behind the multiheaded beast of her feelings about herself and her past as a girl and a daughter is a backdrop of yearning thrown up by this woman's mentions of her films. She ignores it over and over, but a dozen times a day, every day, every week for five years, she has wished for a brief escape into the perfect satisfaction of using this mess—this crazy tangle of childhood memory and shame and self-righteousness and hope and fear—to create a character (utterly real but blessedly pretend) who can tell a story that will make others not just weep (she has done that before) but also understand. *Understand!* And (as if that in itself wouldn't be enough) afterward clap, stand up, go home, and never think of her again.

"Are you still there, dear?"

"What? I'm sorry—"

"Mrs. Lippincott said she felt she had no choice but to call Animal Control. There's a notice on the door now. They're coming by tomorrow to pick her up unless somebody comes and claims her."

Akhil's palms are flat on the counter, as if to hold the whole kitchen in place.

Jessica says, "Do you know what hospital my father is in?"

"Summerlin, I should think. But if you don't mind my asking, how could you not have known about this? Have you been on location somewhere, dear? Somewhere remote?"

3

Spiders

The third is much younger, just a girl standing that night in a T-shirt and panties in front of an open refrigerator in North Las Vegas, eating squares of deli ham from a partitioned package—crackers, circles of turkey, stars of yellow cheese. The top shelf makes almost a halo behind her—a stick of butter, the blue-white ceiling above, a gallon of Sunny Delight. She brushes the blond hair from her damp forehead with the back of her wrist, chewing. The kitchen is small, with white-linoleum floors and chipped white formica counters, and through the dormer window above the sink, she can see the asphalt tile roof of another section of the same building. There are two sounds: from down the hall a din of rushing water—strangely amplified like the crash of some interior waterfall—and through the tiny open window, the metronome bark of another neglected dog.

This is Vivian.

She looks at a doorway at the end of a narrow neck of hall.

She looks at the clock on the stove: 7:15.

On the scratched surface of the metal folding table a pink cell phone studded with glittering rhinestones begins ringing. She closes the refrigerator door and takes a *People* magazine from the counter behind it and tosses it over the ringing phone. The cover is divided into quadrants, each with a different movie-star mother playing with one of her children: at the top of a playground slide; running after ducks; reading under a tree; laughing over ice cream on a bench. On the stove sits an empty saucepan and a kettle beside it. She gives the kettle a little lift to check it for water, and turns on the burner underneath. Out on the roof a pigeon lands with an airy flap of wings, silent beneath the sound of rushing water from a room beyond the kitchen, and now the cell phone ringing, and still that bark, and bark, and bark of a dog. She watches the pigeon flap again, veering along the tiles to the ridge of another dormer, where it poops. The magazine jiggles a bit each time the phone rings. Finally the phone stops ringing and she eats a star of cheese, waiting, and when the phone chirps out its single beep she flips the magazine off it to look in the little window. "Vivian's Phone." One missed call and five voice mails.

Then a baby begins to cry.

She looks again at the hallway.

A second baby's cry rises in concert with the first.

She is still holding the magazine when she enters the little room. It is a slant-ceilinged place with a swaybacked queen-sized bed and a milk crate for a nightstand with a box of condoms on top. On the floor at the foot of the bed are her own things—a little gray white-noise machine roaring a steady blanket of static, a pair of liquor cartons full of her clothes, and in the corner, in a small closet beneath a row of men's track suits on hangers, tucked behind a collection of new-looking basketball shoes, two tiny slouch-spined babies in mismatched infant car seats on the cracked linoleum floor. Both babies are wailing—red-faced, bald but for a peach-fuzzing of white hair, one dressed in a pink T-shirt and the other in blue—but what draws Vivian's eye, what grabs her attention despite all that movement and anguish, is the still figure of a large shiny black spider on the white plastic handle of the girl's carrier.

The babies are too small to have feared or even noticed it, of course. They're just crying, but as they cry and kick, they jiggle their carriers, and the spider's forward leg gives a slow exploratory twitch. Vivian reaches down and picks up one of the basketball shoes and very slowly and steadily, with her hand trembling as she reaches, she crushes the spider against the handle with the sole of the shoe.

For a few seconds she holds it there, frozen. The babies scream beneath her outstretched arm. Then she reaches the magazine out and slides it under the shoe, drawing it toward her between the babies, and flips the shoe over to see the mess that's left—a tangle of crushed legs and a flattened black body with a red hourglass at its center.

The kettle in the kitchen begins to scream now too, but Vivian walks steadily toward the kitchen and sets the shoe and magazine on the table. She pours the kettle water into the saucepan, quieting it. Then she opens a cupboard and takes out a can of formula and a pair of nursing bottles.

Later the bottles sit empty on a coffee table in a tiny, steepled living room, and the babies lie happily on a pink fleece blanket on the linoleum floor. The water sound is gone, and without it the sound of barking is louder. Vivian is sitting on the back of the sofa with her arm out the dormer window, smoking. She has a short yellow satin robe on now over her T-shirt, and with each bark she flinches. Then she hears a key in the door.

The man who comes through it is a little older, but young too, dark-skinned, lean, wearing a shiny red track suit and silver basketball sneakers. He has a plastic grocery bag and from it he pulls a fresh pack of cigarettes and a box of Twizzlers and tosses them on the coffee table.

"For you," he says. "How's my lady?"

"Marco—"

"Hold up. There's more." He reaches down into the bag and pulls out a black waxed-paper box, the kind restaurants use for leftovers, and a bottle of nail polish the color of cotton candy. He kneels down on the linoleum in front of the sofa. "Let me fix you up. Then you have some steak. I know how my lady love steak."

He unscrews the long black cap on the bottle of polish. In the shadow of the upturned white collar on his jacket is a track of five scars, pale and small and round such as the tip of a cigarette makes, so evenly spaced they look strung there, like beads.

"Marco," she says.

"This pink looked just like you," he says. He draws the brush out and strokes it along the nail on her big toe.

"Marco, I have to show you something."

"What is it, baby?"

"It was in the bedroom. There was a spider."

"Aw. I wish I been here to get it for you. That's no job for a lady."

"The poisonous kind."

"You needed your man around to get it. Isn't that what I told you I'd do when I found you?"

"It was a black widow, I think."

"All puff up and scared and lonely in your bitty car in the parking lot at the mall?"

"The kind with the red shape on its back."

"I said, 'Come back with me, I change my mind, no way do I care you're pregnant. Backseat of a Pinto no place for a lady to live. I'll take care of you.' Next time you save the spiders for Marco, baby. I'll get them for you."

"I think we should call the exterminator."

"Sure thing," he says, drawing the brush out of the bottle. "Anything for my girl."

"Do you know one?"

"You just leave it to Marco. I'll take care of everything." He applies the polish to the smallest toes, one by one, with careful fingers.

She says, "Or I could look one up in the phone book? I could call myself?"

"That's no job for a lady like you. It my job to take care of you. Didn't I say so?" He blows on her toes. "Now, how about those babies? They need anything? I'm about to go out again."

"Some more formula maybe."

"Diapers?"

"Sure," she says.

"You got it." He blows again on her nails. "You stay here and play games on that pretty sparkly phone I got for you. I just be gone a couple hours. I got to meet two business associates of mine tonight. Then I'm going to bring them back here with me, and I need to ask you one more time to do me a favor."

He blows again, gently.

Vivian is looking at the top of his head. There is a thin spot near the crown where she can see one more of those long-ago burns. She says, "Those same guys who own this building?"

"No, that was just for once with them. These guys are just business associates. I got to do business, baby. Where you think I get money to buy those fancy chairs your babies sleep in?"

Vivian taps her ash out the window. "Okay," she says.

"Be about midnight probably."

"Okay."

"So maybe you have those babies out of the bedroom then."

"Sure."

"They not always quiet even in this room, so you see what you can do. Maybe put them out on the flat part of the roof like I did before."

"Sure, Marco."

Then he opens the door and shuts it behind him.

Vivian puts out her cigarette on a roof tile and climbs off the couch. In the kitchen cupboard, next to a formula can, a bag of potato chips, and a bottle of Cutty Sark, is a very old phone book. She takes her little pink cell phone from the table next to his white shoe on the magazine and she pages through it: Eviction, Excavating, Extermination: see Pest Control.

By the time she hears the knock on the door, she has put on more clothes—a white sundress with peach-colored flowers, red flip-flops, and a navy blue zip-up sweatshirt with a hood. The babies are drifting off on her two shoulders, one in pink-footed pajamas and the other in blue, and she is doing a soft jiggle step until she can be sure they are fully asleep.

She dances to the door and crouches down almost to kneeling to keep her torso upright as she turns the dead bolt. "Come in," she says.

The door opens and there stands a white-haired man wearing a blue work jumpsuit, leaning over to slide a heavy-looking black duffel bag through the door. "You called Animal Control yet about that dog?"

"It's my boyfriend's."

"He ever take it for a walk?"

"He got it as a guard dog."

"You ask me, a man ought to take care of the things he uses," he says, still struggling with the bag, and then he stands upright and gets a first full look at her in her flowered sundress and rubber sandals, a baby sleeping on each shoulder. He coughs, bringing a fist to his mouth. "Twins?" he says.

She nods.

"My sisters were twins. They lost the same teeth within hours of each other for every blessed tooth in their mouths. In their teens, just before the phone would ring, one would say, 'Answer the phone, Ma. It's Kara calling to get picked up early from band practice.' Magic. You've got twenty pounds of magic there sleeping split between your shoulders."

Vivian's heart lifts. Before she can think what to say, he cocks his head and wrinkles his brow again. "You forget some water running somewhere?"

"It's white noise. To help them sleep through the barking."

"I see." The patch on his jumpsuit says "Harold." He picks up his bag. "So. Where's your crawl space?"

Vivian cocks her head, thinking. "I'm not sure. I found the spider in the back bedroom there where we sleep. Besides that there's just this room and the kitchen."

"Let's try the kitchen," he says.

From the threshold he looks the little white-on-white space up and down a second. Then he sets his bag on the floor and muscles the refrigerator out into the center of the room, revealing a thick black cord, a furring of dust at the baseboard, and a small cupboard door cut into the wall.

"Bingo."

He fishes a pair of gloves and a carpenter's white face mask out of his bag and puts them on. Then he switches on a flashlight, swings open the cupboard, and disappears into the dark of the hole. Vivian creeps down the hall and lays the two babies sleeping in their infant carriers, and by the time she steps back into the kitchen he is already backing out again.

He sits down heavily in her vinyl-covered kitchen chair and yanks down his face mask, his eyes wide with surprise. "Do you have any Scotch?"

He looks stricken.

Vivian opens the cupboard and takes out the big jug of Cutty Sark. She pours it into a juice glass, and the man drains it and sets the empty glass on the table with a thunk. "Now then," he says. "Do you have any friends you can stay with?"

"Friends?"

"What I want you to do is take your babies and leave."

"Leave?"

"Go to a motel for a few nights."

Vivian blinks at him.

"Never in thirty years have I seen anything like what is in your crawl space. It's"—he squeezes his eyes shut and then opens them wide and shakes his head—"it's like Hell's own nest in there. Spiders on top of spiders. I've never seen so many in one space in all my days."

"Can't you get rid of them?"

"'Course I can. It'll be the job of a lifetime, but I can do it. What I'm saying is meantime this is no place for you and those babies. It's like something out of the Old Testament. A B-movie nightmare. You get out of this place, do you hear?"

·   ·   ·

The babies are still sleeping in the white-noise-filled room as she packs. The space is lit with moonlight through the two dormers, and a little clip lamp shines on the condoms from the headboard of the bed. She closes the flaps of each of the liquor cartons and carries them softly one by one out into the hall, and then down the stairs and out into the street at night where his dog is still barking. A bark like the ticking of some slow clock.

Her car is an old brown Pinto with a stripped metal hood parked in front of the hydrant and a plank fence with a furring of weedy grass below. As she hefts the boxes into the hatchback the barking continues, so queer and regular, and she leaves the door open, like a wide mouth yawning, to step to the fence and peer between the slats.

A German shepherd dog. Black and brown with soft-looking ears. He looks up at the yellow windows of the attic apartment, his body recoiling like a gun as he releases each of his barks. The brown grass is long and matted and covered with his turds. In one corner is a whole bag of kibble torn open, and a pile of the brown food pebbles lies mounded in the dirt. He barks again. Vivian steps away and closes the back of her car and hurries back up the stairs.

In the kitchen she mixes two bottles of formula and slips the can of powder and the bottles into a dirty yellow backpack with black straps. She slips in the glittery little phone and the *People* magazine too. And her cigarettes in a zipper pouch with flowers. In the bedroom she unplugs the white noise, and in the sudden quiet, she wraps the cord around the machine and looks at her babies. The girl lies with her arm slung above her head like a dancer, and the boy keeps his arms flat at his sides like a doll. The dog barks, a sharp report now in the silent room, and both babies stiffen. Vivian checks her watch—11:15.

Outside she sets the carriers on the backseat. As she fiddles with their safety buckles they stir, but they do not wake, and when the boy begins to whimper, struggling against her, she smooths a wisp of his hair from his forehead. She tests the straps with two fingers and straightens the clip. She laces the car's seat belts through the slits on each carrier and leans down on the back of each one with the heel of her left hand as she buckles to make sure they will be tight. Then she stands back and takes a deep breath in the dark street. The dog is still barking, but there are stars above and the lighted windows around are just shapes. No one she knows anywhere nearby except these babies.

She gets in behind the wheel and takes a little pink Velcro wallet out of her backpack. She opens it up and takes out the bills to count them. Fourteen dollars. She turns the ignition key and watches the needle on the gas gauge rise to a quarter tank. Then she pulls away, driving out past two blocks of houses with their chain-link fences and garbage-filled yards, past the Popeye's and the Kmart and the Poker Palace to an open frontage road that runs parallel to a highway bearing south. Once she has merged, she turns on the radio, not too loud, to something soft and heartfelt with just a strand of guitar and a lone girl singing.

4

Strays

The last is an older woman. Soft gray curls twining down into a lengthy braid. Eyes a popsicle blue. She stands alone in her barn coat by a window looking out over an empty plain of creosote bush and dry red-brown soil and one distant barn beneath a strip of bright blue sky in the barren scrublands of southern Nevada.

On the wooden workbench she is taking plastic tube vials of flea treatment from a case box. Her left hand is a bulb of flesh-colored plastic topped with a pair of steel loops. She grips with these and cuts the tops off the vials with a pair of scissors in a good right hand knuckled over with turquoise-and-silver rings, and then adds them to a long line, propped a little, tips up, against the wooden backsplash—fifteen of them maybe; more than twenty when she finishes. Then she slits the bottom of the box with a razor and flattens it down on the concrete floor with her high green rubber boots.

Coming through the low doorway out of the garage, she steps into a living room split down the middle with white plastic baby fencing. Inside the fence line the gold shag rug is covered in a thick clear plastic tarp and crawling with yellow puppies, plus a heavy-teated mother dog asleep in a whelping box in the corner next to an old white-painted coffee table with bite-spindled legs. She passes on into a tiny dark front hall and then into a bright small kitchen, calling out, "Charlene?"

The kitchen is clean. A drying rack bears a single clean pan and a blue-and-white enamel mug turned upside down and white-and-yellow curtains framing another view of that barn on the plain.

She opens the kitchen door onto a half-acre rectangle of dry dirt yard fenced in with chain-link and filled with grown dogs of every type and measure. Wrestling and playing, tugging at shreds of toweling, digging holes, just sleeping in the sun, or running. And barking: sharp and quick, low and even, growls and bays and little yelps like the squeaks of a squeezed toy. A good half of them leave their occupations to crowd her, and she pats them, talking to them in a singsong voice, saying, "Aren't you an angel?" and "That's a good cutie," and spurning the ones who jump up on her coat by crossing her arms and saying, "Not a bit of that, mister" in a flat lower voice like the one she'd used to call the girl.

This is Lynn.

She stumbles a bit among the dogs, her boots invisible in the tangle, until she slips out, blocking them with her knees, through a chain-link door leading into a big rutted turnaround, and she cups her silver-ringed hand to the side of her mouth. "Charlene!"

She visors her eyes and then looks around the circle, at her porched house and garage, and two shed buildings opposite, and in the distance a brown barn with a tin roof, and finally down the long drive. It is there at the far end of it, near where the gravel thins and meets the highway, that she sees it: a truck with a little exhaust coming out the back.

She sets off in her green boots, her hands stuffed in the pockets of her coat. Her long braid swings a bit across the back of it, and as she gets close she can see a young boy at the wheel and next to him a dark-haired young girl. They are talking intensely. The young girl looks into the boy's eyes and nods. Even when this older woman, Lynn, gets right up next to the truck, so close she can hear the country music inside the rolled-up windows, the girl doesn't see her.

Lynn taps on the boy's window with her metal loops.

He wheels around, and the girl looks up. The boy's mouth gapes a little, and he rolls the window down, cranking with his arm and revealing the heartfelt music—a girl's voice and an earnest single strand of guitar.

"Sorry, Lynn," the girl says.

"What for? For sitting in a truck a minute with a boy and a radio?"

The girl shifts her eyes at the boy.

The boy looks down in his lap.

Lynn cocks her head. "No, I didn't bet so. Is there something else then?"

"Yes," the girl says.

Lynn waits.

The girl slips her hand into the boy's. Lynn sees a duffel bag now on the floor. And on the dashboard, a map.

The girl raises her chin and in a voice she might have practiced says, "Bobby and me have a dream we need to follow."

"Oh?"

"We're going to Los Angeles. To be actors in a restaurant near Disneyland."

Lynn nods. She sees now that the map on the dash is not a map of Nevada but of California.

She watches the girl's eyes cut past her toward the dogs in the distance. The girl lowers her chin. In a less certain voice she says, "I can wait, though. Until you find someone to help out with the dogs."

Lynn shakes her head. "No call for that. You know how I do."

"You'll be okay, you mean?"

"Come here," Lynn says. She beckons with her good right hand. "Come here out of that truck."

The girl darts a look at the boy, who gives a little shrug and looks back down at his lap. She gets out of the car and walks to the older woman, crunching the gravel in her cowboy boots with a miniskirt above them, her hands stuffed deep in her puffy down coat.

Lynn gives her a hug, just a quick squeeze, and then lets her go. "I can see you worried over telling me. I'm happy for you, couldn't you have guessed I would be?"

Later in the chain-link yard, Lynn pets each dog first a good long while before kneeling beside it and hugging it around the neck with her arm with the loops for a hand. She has the open flea-treatment vials set standing up in the hollows of a partitioned liquor carton beside her, and she takes them out one at a time, spilling it into the fur between each dog's shoulder blades. It takes a long time. When she is finished she takes a break, standing in the kitchen doorway watching them, clasping a plastic hummus tub in the metal loops and dipping a piece of bread into it with her hand while the sun sinks lower in the sky. Her eyes drift off toward the distant barn and its long shadow, and her face dulls, but then some of the dogs come up and sniff the air beneath her snack, and she smiles and shakes her head, chewing. One sets a paw gently on her boot. She laughs and wipes her lips with the back of her wrist. "You're next." Her voice is high and loose again. "You're next I promise, sweet sillies, do I ever forget about you?"

And she doesn't. Over the next hour, she rolls the cans out into the turnaround in the failing light—big cans, the size of cooking pots—and makes a line of twenty bowls, and as night begins to fall she takes a little flashlight from her coat pocket and holds it between her teeth.

It is fully dark when she slips into the cab of her truck. She is still wearing her work clothes, and when she starts the engine, the light from the dashboard reveals the sleeves of her coat to be streaked with something dark. She reaches across herself to pull the door shut with her good hand and heads down her long gravel drive and out through the empty land along the state highway toward the town lights in the distance. It is not a big town. She pulls into a full lot next to a gas station and a building beside it with a high sign above that says COPLEY'S. Inside next to a single cash register are a few rows of grocery items and then some diner booths beyond with a sizzling kitchen on the way other side. Lynn goes to the chip aisle and grabs two shallow pull-top cans of black bean dip.

The woman at the register has an updo of hair dyed the buff color of bandaids, and she sits on a stool filing her nails. There is a bulletin board behind her fringed with notes and flyers and a few canceled checks, and on the counter next to the register sit a bowl of peppermint candies, a March of Dimes donation can, and a rack of *People* magazines, the one with mothers and children on the cover.

"Got something for your board, Ruth Ann," Lynn says. She sets down the bean dip and takes an index card and pen from her tote.

Ruth Ann looks up from her nails to watch her write.

*Room and all meals (vegetarian) daily in exchange for
light work. Three Paws Dog Rescue.*

Ruth Ann says, "Lord—one of your girls ever last longer than three months?"

"Only in the bruise on my ass."

Ruth Ann snorts. She punches the keys on the register, holding a bean can up and away from her eyes. "Not a bit in your heart too, though?"

"Nah."

"I don't believe it. All that time you spend together?"

Lynn is still looking down, adding her phone number to the card. "Trick is to keep it simple. Bringing up poop duty nips most any serious conversation in the bud."

"*Tch!*" She bats a hand. "I don't believe you for an instant."

"—Who's got fleas and who's off his food. Tough to knit a sweater out of snippets." She straightens and hands her the card.

"Nonsense. Those girls love you."

"Like a bag of chips, maybe."

"They love you every bit as much as the boys your folks took in for the milking season loved the two of them."

"Well, that's just stretching things and you know it. My folks were the best there was. Either one of them was worth six of me."

"Marla's girl told me she was going to start a shelter like you after she finishes at State."

"Poor dear."

"She wrote her college essay about you."

"Mixup in the admissions office, I guess."

"Sounds to me like you gave up some heart real estate."

"I got dogs for my heart space."

Ruth Ann takes the card and twists on her stool to pull a tack from the board. "They leave you too, Lynn Doran! You've made it your livelihood for them to leave!"

"Fair enough." She licks a finger and counts out the money for the bean dip. "But a dog never chooses to go."

Across the room near the grill a cheer goes up. Ruth Ann glances over to see a cluster of truckers high-fiving each other over a table strewn with sugar packets, but Lynn goes on counting change.

Ruth Ann studies her.

"So what are you going to do?"

"I'll manage."

"It's ten o'clock and I know for a fact you just finished your chores because you still smell like Alpo."

"Maybe that's just my natural smell."

"Look at you, it's all over your coat, even. And I bet that's with a half day of help before she bolted too, isn't it?"

Lynn shrugs.

"What are you going to do days you have a vet run or pickup to do?"

"Easy, Chicken Little."

"Well, tell me then. Name a single idea."

Lynn slides the money across the counter. "I'll get Johnny or Bob to stop over if I get in a bind."

"Both of them have construction jobs now, and you know it."

"Another girl will come along."

"There aren't more than thirty in the whole county, and every one of them that hasn't already quit you has a warm bed and parents with a full can of marbles."

Lynn points at the register, and Ruth Ann rolls her eyes and punches a button, popping the cash drawer open.

She licks a finger and starts counting out bills. "Tell me this at least. If I come by on Saturday myself to shovel shit and slop the dogs will you at least put on a clean jacket and come out to the Railhead with me?"

"The artichoke dip at the Railhead tastes like cat food."

"I admit it would be an adjustment. All the guys you danced with last time you came out with me work the floor in walkers now."

"Now you see why I save all my dancing for my big nights on the strip."

Ruth Ann puts her hand with the change on one hip. "All right, a movie then."

"Maybe."

"Because I can't come in for any more of your tea and green smoothies. A girl like me prefers pay in beer or movie candy."

Lynn smiles.

"And a laugh, for God's sake," Ruth Ann says, handing her the change finally. "It's like a crypt over there the way you keep it. It gives me the creeps."

To Lynn the house is a bright spot she can see from the dark of the road, and she turns and follows the twin beams of her truck lights down the dirt-and-gravel drive. The dogs greet her with their barking, and she calls out, "Hey now. Hush now, ladies and gents," and she clomps up the porch steps in her boots and removes them inside so she is in her sock feet.

In the garage, in the corner, is a wall of shelves stacked with flattened boxes. She takes a smallish one, and she crisscrosses the bottom flaps to make it—a box their heartworm pills came in that says "Heartgard" along the side. Then she takes it through the living room to a pair of double doors that stand open to a room too dark to see.

She flips a switch. A king-sized bed with two windows flanking and two matching nightstands holding fringed lamps, and a bathroom with double sinks beyond. A master bedroom once. Lynn sees that the girl made the bed before she left, with the yellow-and-black star quilt smoothed down and the pillows fluffed, but there are traces. A hair clip on the nightstand. A pair of socks balled up near the skirt of the bed. A tube of watermelon lip gloss on top of the dresser. And on the biggest wall two posters—one of a group of three boys with their arms crossed and one of a girl alone with a guitar—with the edges of some older ones sticking out from underneath.

Lynn sets the little box on the nightstand. First she takes fresh sheets from the bottom drawer of the dresser, and she changes the bed, gripping the edges in her different hands in different ways and smoothing it down and covering it again with the black-and-yellow star quilt. Then she gathers the girl's stray things, setting them in the bottom of the little box—the hair clip and the socks and the lip gloss. She takes a marker from a drawer in the nightstand beneath and across the side she writes, "Charlene." Behind a louvered closet door is an empty hanging rod and a high shelf above it with a row of other boxes, each labeled with a name: "Karlee," "Amber," "Cecelia," "Jessie." Lynn places this new one at the end beside them and closes the door.

The room upstairs where she herself sleeps is hardly a bedroom at all—just a narrow corduroy-covered daybed bullied into a corner by an enormous oak pedestal desk. The surface of the old desk is furred with dust and heaped with file boxes and a black sewing machine so old it looks to be an antique. Lynn takes her coat off and lays it over the back of the desk chair. Her mechanical hand has a cable running up the side to a harness that loops around the back of her shoulders. She shrugs the straps off and pulls the hand free so that there is just the smooth bulb of her wrist, and then she takes off the rest of her clothes and puts on a plain long cotton nightgown from a hook on the back of the door.

At the end of the upper hallway is a closed door she does not open or even meet with her eyes. She steps into a tiny low-ceilinged bathroom and washes her face with one hand and brushes her teeth without watching herself in the mirror and returns to her room and piles both arm bolsters from the daybed next to the desk and pulls back the buckling corduroy spread. She slips in under it, sitting up against the bolsters without dimming the lights or drawing the curtains, and takes a book of sudoku from a pile on the desk and opens a marked page. Then she slides open the bottom desk drawer and takes out a sealed manila envelope, a clean juice glass, and an empty fifth bottle of Jack Daniel's, and sets them there on top beside the stack of puzzles.

Day 2

5

Unwanted Callers

The empty bottle and the empty glass still sit clean and empty beside the envelope when she wakes. Moonlight through the uncurtained window shows them to be so. Lynn switches on a lamp, throwing shadows. She is out of bed quickly, standing among them and casting one herself, pulling on blue jeans and a thermal shirt and fitting her wrist into the plastic-and-metal hand. She slips her other arm through the harness strap like a sweater. The clamp on this hand is closed unless she puts tension on the cable to open it. She does this by reaching out, stretching her arm against the harness on her body, and when she relaxes again it always closes.

The house is silent. The dogs have not yet figured her to be awake. But soon she is creaking down the stairs, and when she reaches the kitchen and flicks a light on, one of them outside yelps.

Then her telephone rings.

She looks at it. A cream-colored cordless on the kitchen table.

She looks at the clock. 6:02.

She picks it up. "Dog rescue."

"Hello?" It's a girl's voice. "Hello, ma'am, I mean? I'm sorry to call so early, but I saw you were awake."

Lynn looks out the window into the dark.

The girl says, "I'm out on the road in my car and I was waiting for the lights to go on. I was calling about your posting at the diner? About the room and the job?"

Lynn squints. She tries to focus out beyond the silhouettes of the dogs stirring in the moonlight. They are barking, and their eyes catch in the light from the kitchen or the moon above, and stare back at her, eerie and hollowed. She can't see anything on the road.

"Well, then," she says. "I guess you better drive on in so I can get a look at you."

She hangs up the phone without waiting for the girl to answer and crosses her arms to watch out the window. A pair of headlights appears in the dark distance and then swings around and comes at her, bouncing down the long gravel drive. The dogs are barking in full now. Lynn passes through the dark, low-ceilinged foyer, just big enough to pull a pair of boots on in, and she does that. Then she flicks on a porch light and steps out to see a small hatchback lumber over the rutted earth to stop in her circle.

The noise of the dogs is like gunfire now—sharp barks overlying one another. A few of them stand on their hind legs at the chain-link wall along the turnaround, their nails tinkling against the metal and making the big wall bow.

"Hush now," Lynn says. "Hush now, boys and girls."

The engine on the little car dies, and the headlights go out. Lynn can't make out anything through the windshield, and the door doesn't open when it should. She doesn't wait more than a second. She backs into the house and reaches into the deep back of the hall closet with her good hand and drags out a liquor carton with a dozen slim tall boxes of Jack Daniel's nestled inside. With her eyes still on the car through the window glass, Lynn flips open the lid of the second box in the back row of four and draws out a pistol.

The dogs are still barking and the car is still dark and closed, and Lynn's eyes are on it through the screen door. She doesn't cock it or take aim, just steps back out onto the porch watching the car jiggle a little with some weighty internal shifting. Then the driver's door swings open, and out tumbles a girl in a sundress and a hooded sweatshirt and the sound of babies bawling.

Right away the girl sees the gun—not pointing at her, just dangling at Lynn's side in her hand—but she raises her hands in the air all the same.

Lynn takes no heed of this. She nods her head at the car, her arms still hanging at her sides. "So is it just you and the baby in there then?"

"Yes. I mean, no. I mean no, ma'am? There's two of them. Two babies, I mean?" A sweet nervous voice rising up and up, like a puff of something.

"You took so long getting out I thought maybe you were up to something."

"I was just trying to quiet them."

"Well, that's a goal I can favor."

The babies are still screaming, and the girl's hands are still up. "I woke them coming down the drive. They didn't sleep so well out there."

"You slept in your car?"

"Yes, ma'am."

The girl's arms are shaking.

"Well, put your hands down and tend to them. Come on now, I'm not even aiming at you. I'll go back inside and put away my gun."

She turns and goes inside, not waiting to see what the girl will do, and she stashes the gun back in the well of the liquor carton and slides it to the back of her closet. She can still hear the babies while she does it, and the dog noise seems steady and almost calm behind their wailing. She stands alone in her hallway, pausing a little longer in the dark closed space before she goes out again to face it.

When she draws near the car, the girl is just backing out of it with the two carriers, holding them by her sides like buckets of water. Two button faces and bunched bodies. How old can they be? They are dark-faced with screaming, but for a single, blissfully relaxing instant, they both stop in the moonlight to hitch in a breath of the fresh, cool air. It falls like the weird sudden quiet under an overpass in a rainstorm. Then they start again. The girl expected this though, apparently. She is kneeling on the rutted earth unbuckling them, snip-snap, and then—how does she do it, even?—she places the carriers right up snug against each other to brace them, scoops an arm under each baby and lifts them up toward each other, cocking her arms out suddenly so that there they are, one in each crook. Right away she starts swaying back and forth, back and forth, one little baby face nestled in each arm of her sweatshirt.

The wailing turns to whimpering, and the babies quiet altogether.

"I'll be damned," Lynn says.

Then from the back of the little brown car comes the sound of ringing, and the girl gets a panicked look in her eyes. Lynn glances at the car, but the girl keeps swiveling at the waist, like a sprinkler head watering.

"I'll just give you a minute," Lynn says turning.

"No, no—" It rings again. "It'll stop soon and go to voice mail, I promise." The babies are winding up again, whimpering and fussing. "Uch. I'm so sorry for all this noise."

Lynn points a thumb over her shoulder at the porch, backing up. "No worries. I'll just—"

"They're good sleepers, I swear. They're not usually like this."

"I'm just going to leave you alone and go—"

Another ring. "I can switch my phone to vibrate as soon as it goes to voice mail. It's been that same caller for days now. I wish they'd stop calling, and they never do."

"I'll just give you some privacy and fix us some—"

"Wait!" The babies begin to cry in full. "This isn't turning out at all like I planned. I meant to be no bother and here my phone is ringing and the babies are crying."

"I'm just going to make coffee," Lynn says.

"But you don't understand. They'll never settle down outside here. They need to eat. You'll come back out with a coffee for me and they'll be screaming and my phone will ring again and then you'll never take me as your boarder, and I'm wondering which is worse—set them down and let you hear them scream even louder so I can make them bottles, or put you to work toting my backpack and mixing the formula yourself so I can keep them a little quieter."

Lynn blinks. The girl is not more than seventeen years old and frank-faced. No streaks in her hair or piercings or dark eyeliner—no costume shows of boredom or sophistication. No armor at all on this girl.

Lynn says, "Better go with me toting and mixing so we can hear each other to talk about the job I have for you. My name's Lynn Doran."

"I'm Vivian Able."

"And the little lady and gentleman?"

"Sebastian and Emmaline."

The phone stops ringing.

"Pleased to make your acquaintances," Lynn says. She circles to the passenger side of the hatchback and reaches in for the girl's black-and-yellow backpack. It beeps as she lifts it.

"Another voice mail," the girl says mournfully, and Lynn turns away from her to lead her inside.

The dogs are still barking, hurling themselves against the chain-link with clangs and sharp reports at random intervals that make the girl flinch, but the babies begin to quiet as she follows Lynn up the porch steps into the house.

Inside, the girl has to walk sideways with her load to pass through doorways—porch to hall, hall to kitchen—and the babies start to whimper again.

Lynn sets the backpack on the counter. "You may have to talk me through the steps," she says.

"The can of powder is in that big main pocket there?"

"You want me to bring it to you?"

"You can just open it."

Lynn stares at the backpack. The weave of the yellow fabric is worn so thin at the bottom she can see the dark shapes of the things inside. There is a stain above the pocket—a dribble of something purple—and near the zipper a slash of ballpoint pen. She swallows thickly. Then she clamps a strap with her two loops and with her ringed fingers slowly unzips it. The contents shift and settle even as the two sides part along the zipper. She looks down inside. A magazine and a glittery little pink cell phone. A pink Velcro wallet. A little zippered pouch with flowers. She glances uncomfortably at the girl. "Looks like it might be under a few things."

"You can pull them out of the way."

"I could hold the babies for you if you'd like to fish it out yourself."

"Just lay them on the table, why don't you?"

Lynn looks back in the bag. Then she does as the girl suggested. She lowers her hand down in and pulls out the magazine and phone. Then the zippered pouch and the wallet. Then the white-noise machine. Then a whole pile of crumpled Kleenex—enough for a whole night of crying—so many the girl laughs. "Sorry about that."

But even then Lynn pretends not to notice, just keeps drawing out the knotted wads of tissue until finally she unearths two empty nursers and the formula can. She eyes the tiny print. The fussing grows stronger, especially the little girl, whose dark eyes blink and squint in the bright.

Vivian says, "First you just heat a kettle of water."

Lynn lights the stove with a long-handled lighter, and Vivian tries to find a spot to pivot, but the kitchen is small, and this places her elbows in the path of the sink and the stove, where Lynn is trying to pass now with the kettle. She holds it high and shimmies past.

Vivian says, "Now you just put one scoop in each bottle and fill them with cold water to the six line on the side." She watches Lynn clamp the rim of the canister with her metal loops. "Is it hard doing things with that hand?"

"Nah," Lynn says. She scoops the powder with her good hand, and Vivian improvises a new rhythm behind her with the babies, dipping one down and then the other, like an oil derrick, taking up less space.

"How did you lose it?"

"Farm accident." She puts the scoop back in the bin. "Now what?"

"Just shake them to mix it a bit. I put a finger over the top of the nipple so it doesn't spray." When Lynn gets this right Vivian says, "What kind of farm accident?"

"Dairy."

"What happened, I meant."

"Crushed it between some broken boards on a platform above the slurry pit," she says, and waggles a bottle at her. "Now I heat these somehow, I guess?"

"That's right. I do it in a pan," Vivian says. "How long ago was it?"

Lynn pours some water from the kettle into a pan and sets the bottles in. "I bet they like quiet when you feed them. Is a bed good?"

"Oh, anywhere, but a big armchair or a couch would be better."

"Let's get you set up while those finish."

Lynn leads her into the living room, where the mother dog is sleeping with her six pups nestled in, and she turns on one soft lamp, bringing in a dim circle of yellow over the flowered seat of the couch. Before she sits, Vivian crouches all the way to kneeling to pinch a yellow throw pillow with the thumb and forefinger on one hand. Using some quick calculus that takes no measurement or reckoning, she drops it a third of the way along the seat cushion and then eases down so that her elbows fall exactly on the pillow and the arm of the couch. The babies open their eyes now and stare at Lynn, and—as if she has disappointed them—begin fussing in unison.

Vivian says, "If you maybe could bring me those bottles now? I bet they're just ready. They get a misted look, and you can test by dribbling a bit on your wrist."

Lynn goes to the kitchen. There in the pan of water, the bottles are just misted as the girl had said they would be, and Lynn tests them and finds they are right. When she brings them back, Vivian simply opens her two hands, the babies still nestled in her arms and whimpering, and Lynn leans to meet her open hands with the two warm bottles. In another trick of competence, Vivian shifts her arms slightly toward center, so that the babies' legs rest on her thighs, the soles of their pajamaed feet almost touching, and she tilts her wrists way back, just reaching their tiny rosebud lips with the bottle nipples. Both babies open their mouths like birds and close their dark eyes and begin to suck. For a few seconds the spell and spectacle of this girl's ease with the babies holds the older woman transfixed. But then perhaps the history behind that, or the intimate privacy of what they are doing, making little sucking sounds, or her own dumb idleness there standing between her and the mama dog nesting her pups—something makes her retreat to the kitchen.

She stands by the window and scoops coffee into a paper filter with her back turned to the tableful of Kleenex and the girl's private things. The walls are papered with twin cherries on pale yellow, darker in places where pictures used to hang, the nail holes still there above them. On the counter next to the coffeemaker is a big black and clear blender and a basket of fruit, and behind it, in the shadow of the cupboard, a set of puzzle books and the dark neck of a bottle. The coffeemaker comes to life, bubbling and sighing steam and a trickle of brown into the pot below, and Lynn reaches into the dark corner and takes a sudoku book and lays it on the counter, fat, with pages curled at the corners from use, and she opens it to halfway through where a pencil marks her place and begins to figure.

When the coffeemaker makes a last series of spitting noises and quiets with a gasp, Lynn fills the blue-and-white mug to the brim. She takes a spoon and stirs, although she has added nothing. The yellow backpack lies empty on the table, and what must be most of what the girl calls important still sits arrayed on Lynn's table by Vivian's own invitation, in a cloud of tissues she had done nothing to try to hide. The zipper on her little pouch is open, plainly exposing the cigarettes inside. Her wallet is the kind with a window on the front, and her pure face stares up at Lynn from the driver's license, smiling in an open way no one ever does at the DMV. Vivian Louise Able. Born June 27, 1995. Seventeen: as young as she had looked to Lynn, but no longer seemed. Lynn clamps the coffee cup in her metal loops and sips at it, returning to her puzzle book, writing numbers in the squares with her shaking hand, and forcing any glances past Vivian's possessions out the window at her dogs, a few sniffing the air for traces of the girl and the babies, others tracing tight circles to lie down again and finish their sleeps, and some still barking their gunshot barks at the memory of her arrival.

It is no more than five minutes before she can hear Vivian in the next room shifting. She rinses her mug in the sink and walks as softly as she can to the threshold where the girl holds the two babies, sleeping.

Lynn lowers her voice. "You can lay them down in there."

"I can just use their carriers."

"There's a clean bed."

"That's nice of you really—"

"It's no trouble."

"It's just—they've never slept anywhere but in those car seats."

Lynn doesn't comment on this. She steps outside onto the porch and down the stairs toward the girl's car, squirrel-brown she sees now in the early morning light, with a bumper sticker on the rear chrome that says "Young Life." The two padded buckets still sit there on the hard ground and she reaches for them, with her ring-covered hand and the metal loops opening, and heads back for the house. One or two dogs stand to look at her, but she is not anything to fuss over this early, they know, and she brings the seats inside and passes between Vivian and the mama dog into the darker dark of the bedroom she cleaned last evening, the sun pushing through between the drawn curtains just enough to shed a little light on the strata of posters left behind by the girls she has lost.

Vivian cups her hands beneath the babies' little thighs and stands and brings them in and slides them in under each handle, their arms windmilling first and their toes straining against the pajama feet before they ease and settle into their curved sleep in the seats. From the pocket of her sweatshirt she takes two sets of plastic measuring spoons and sets them on their bellies for them to find when they wake. Then she follows Lynn to her kitchen.

· · ·

Vivian sits at the table heaped with Kleenex, her feet in the red flip-flops hooked behind the spindle legs of one of the old woman's chairs. The white-noise machine lies on its back among her things, its cord still wound tight around it. It is light now through the panes of glass, and she is watching Lynn at the counter stuffing leathery leaves of kale into the clear plastic blender. She steadies a bunch of spinach with her loops of metal and twists and tears off a handful from the pretty white roots and stuffs these in too. A cable pulls the metal loops open and closed. She pins an avocado to a wooden board and slices around it with a big knife and squeezes it free of its pit and then empties the mess of creamy yellow-green in on top. A handful of blueberries. A whole banana. And then she twists open a cloudy jug of apple juice and pours it in over everything. The brown juice trickles down as she lays the rubber lid on top and punches the button with her thumb, setting the blender whirring loudly and clouding with white and bubbles and little pieces that soon disappear. Vivian watches, sipping her coffee, and Lynn watches too, her back to Vivian under the cover of a noise too loud for talking over, until it shuts off on its own, silent now, and full to the brim with pale green.

"Breakfast," Lynn says.

Lynn pours it into two glasses, so thick. When she sets one down in front of her, Vivian thanks her and watches her take a long drink and then set it down and wipe at the corners of her mouth with thumb and ringed forefinger, still standing. "I have to go off in a while to pick up a dog at a shelter about an hour's drive from here. I'll teach you a couple things before I go, and you can rest while I'm gone."

"You mean I can stay?"

"'Course you can."

Vivian's eyes fill. She laughs nervously and wipes them.

Lynn turns her back and cranks the faucet on.

Behind her Vivian says, "I thought you wouldn't want to take me with the babies."

"You kidding?" She picks up a sponge and begins rinsing the blender. "You're a better bet with them. There's no harder worker than a single mom."

"But I thought you'd have questions about me at least."

"Lord, no."

"You don't want to know anything?"

"Not a bit of my business. And I'll thank you not to ask me any more questions either. All we need to know about each other is who fed the dogs." She is busying herself with the blender, soaping it to cut through the avocado and then rinsing it and setting it upside down in the drying rack. When she turns, Vivian is looking down into her full green glass.

Lynn says, "The diner in town serves burgers at lunch and bacon at breakfast."

"This is better for me, I'm sure," the girl says, still gazing at it.

Lynn reaches across the pile of used tissues to grab the glass. "I'll put it in the fridge for you for later. We'd better get started outside."

She loans the girl a pair of rubber boots and an old brown canvas barn coat then, and she leads her for the first time into the dog yard. The dogs rush them and crowd, barking and sniffing at their knees, a couple jumping up with their muddy paws on their coats.

"Oh!" Vivian says, and "Hello there!," laughing and petting the big dogs who jump up to sniff her face.

Lynn says, "First thing is, you have to turn away when they do what you don't want, and only pet them when they do what you like."

"Okay," Vivian says, laughing nervously. The paws of an old yellow Lab are up on one shoulder of her coat.

"You can cross your arms too, to say no."

Vivian crosses her arms, and the Lab slips but jumps up again.

Lynn says, "And if they keep at you, you can walk away."

They start to walk then, with the pack of dogs crowding them, tripping on one another, and Lynn and Vivian tripping too, both of them laughing a bit, but Lynn knowing which dogs she can reach and pet and talk to in a high sweet voice and when to say, "Hey now, not a bit of that, mister," flat and low. When they get to the far side, she opens another door in the chain-link a crack, waving Vivian through while she blocks the dogs with her knees, and then passes through herself, walking backward to keep them from coming with her.

"There's not much to any of this, really," she says. "Just watch how I do and you'll learn it straightaway."

There is a row of water troughs along the driveway, and she walks the fence line now and reaches through the chain-link to unscrew a drain cap, stepping back from the gurgle and splash of water onto the muddy red-brown dirt.

Vivian says, "What's wrong with the dog you're going to pick up?"

"Not a thing. She's just been at the shelter for more than a year, and it's a kill shelter. She's blind, and that makes most people think a dog can't get by."

"Can it, though?"

"Sure, you'll see. Most it takes a few days of bumping into things before they have a layout in their heads. Our pen is a rectangle, and nothing in it but other dogs that have a smell and make noise, so most likely the only thing she'll bump into is the hose bib in the middle there."

She points at a pipe rising up out of a low place in the center of the yard. Three dogs are crowded in around it, digging. "No matter how many times I fill it in with sand they dig it out again." Their heads are bowed, low and purposeful over their work, just touching now and then as their forepaws churn and the loose sand flies out steadily behind them.

She unscrews another drain cap and steps back from the flow of old water.

Vivian says, "Can the other dogs tell if a dog is blind?"

"Some can. Some will help it out by barking to warn him. Like before a car coming down the drive makes noise, and you'll see one of the dogs go right next to a blind one and bark."

"That's sweet."

"Does as much good for the one who does the helping, I think," Lynn says.

All the troughs are empty now, and Lynn pulls the green hose, yanking and dragging it to get it up out of itself where it's coiled near the shed, and she puts the nozzle into the first trough. At the squeak of the faucet handle cranking, a few more dogs get up and come over to nose into the trough. The bottom of the trough starts to fill, the clean fresh water running down the side in a clear sheet, and right away the dogs begin drinking.

Then from the pocket of Lynn's borrowed barn coat, Vivian's cell phone rings.

"Uch," she says. "I'm so sorry I forgot to switch off the ringer."

Lynn turns toward her battered yellow truck. "You can finish this. I better get going."

"It's just that same caller again."

"If I'm gone past two, you might as well feed them. There are cans of meat in the garage, and you can bring them out here and open five and divide them up in twenty-four bowls. They go between that double layer of fence, and then there's a way to raise it when you're ready. You'll see."

Vivian is looking down at her phone. "I don't know why they don't stop."

"The mama dog and pups get a mix of puppy food and milk replacer from under the kitchen sink. You can mix it with warm water in the blender."

"Just ringing and ringing half the time when I'm feeding the babies. Wouldn't you give up if someone never answered? Would you ever just keep calling a person like that?"

Lynn opens the door to her truck and slips in. "And there probably won't be any visitors. Most people will call first on the house phone if they're interested in finding a dog, but every once in a while we get a drop-in. If that happens, you tell them you can show them the dogs, but they'll have to come back for a matching interview with Lynn."

Vivian's phone stops ringing, and she looks at it despairingly. "There's going to be another voice mail." She stands right next to her but does not look up at Lynn behind the wheel of the truck she will leave in. "It's about to give that beep."

"Vivian," Lynn says. She says it sharply, and waits for the girl to look up at her from her sparkly pink phone.

When she does, she has a stricken look.

Lynn says, "I'm not your mother, or your guidance counselor, or your lonely neighbor lady with the after-school cookies."

Vivian blinks.

Lynn says, "You don't owe me any confessions." She reaches across herself with her good hand to grasp the door handle, ready to shut it. "All the business we need to have in common is those dogs."

When Lynn slams the door and starts her engine, Vivian's phone beeps in her pocket. She watches from the turnaround until the truck is gone down the drive and disappears out of view a half mile or so down the highway. Then she takes the phone out and sees that there are now six messages waiting.

After she fills the last two troughs, Vivian takes stock of her surroundings. Lynn's plot is big, bordered around with barbed-wire fencing at such a vast neighborless distance that Vivian is not even sure where it ends. Next to the house is an attached garage, and the smaller shed where Lynn got the hose, and next to that a plank-and-wire corral where it seems some other animals might once have lived, and in the faraway across the turnaround a long barn with metal walls and roof. She notices a pattern of holes on the corral post near the hose bib, and a few rusty tin cans in the weedy grass behind with holes in them too, and deeper down a scattering of brass-colored shells. She crouches to pick one up, and she slips it into her pocket—not the pocket of Lynn's borrowed coat, but inside, into the patch of the sweatshirt that is her own.

Then she sets off for the barn. Her borrowed boots make a hard sound on the dried mud, scratching here and there through patches of scabby weed, and her heart beats faster as she nears it, its windows boarded over with plywood and its doors too, so that she has to walk around it, the blood pulsing in her ears, to find an opening. When she reaches the far side she sees a strange circle in the earth, a ring of concrete like the rim of a cistern, but flush with the earth and long ago filled in with dirt. Beside it are two big sheets of plywood nailed up to the metal barn walls, one of them hanging askew, and Vivian slips in through the crack.

The only light inside is filtered in through the gaps whoever boarded the openings left. When her eyes adjust, she sees that she is in the remains of what she guesses right away must once have been a small dairy operation. There are drains in the floor, and short sections of gate to make stalls, and in the corner a mostly empty platform that still bears one stainless-steel vat. The concrete is thick with years of dry dirt that has blown beneath the plywood. Silent. Deserted. It gives the place a ghostly feel, but she's still calm enough, until she looks up and sees that overhanging all the steel rafters are the ratty tufts of birds' nests, dozens of them. It is at this sign of life thriving in the graveyard that her pulse starts to race, as if she anticipates the explosion that suddenly bursts from above, flapping wings and wheeling down to the floor just in front of her, raising devils of dust and making her scream. They settle in their places as if to nest there. Just a clutch of wild brown birds with pure white breasts.

Vivian raises a hand to her heart. Then she slips out between the boards and takes off at a run back to Lynn's house. She pauses on the top step when she gets there, her ear cocked for any sound from her babies inside, but there is none. Instead she hears a crunch of tires coming down the drive.

She looks up to see a mud-spattered white pickup jacked up high on its suspension, with big lights on top of the cab. When the door opens, a dog hops out first—a sweet brown-and-black coonhound who bolts for the chain-link to sniff at the other dogs. The yard cranks up with barking, but the oldest dogs stay asleep under the shelter at the far end, nestled against one another like a puzzle of tiles Vivian once saw in a picture.

A man in a camouflage hunting jacket and an orange cap jumps down from the seat. He cocks his head and takes a toothpick from his mouth. He grins.

"You sure as hell ain't Lynn."

He has to raise his voice a bit to carry to her. She is a few yards from him up on the porch.

"Can I help you?" she says.

"I just bet you can."

Vivian backs up a step, so that she is standing in front of the door. "I meant, what did you come for?"

"What's your hurry? You're supposed to say, 'Hi, nice to meet you' first."

She crosses her arms. "Lynn says if you're interested in a dog, you're going to have to come back for a matching interview."

He laughs, taking off his orange cap. Thin pale hair flies up on top in the breeze. "I don't need any more dogs. 'Fact I got another one in back I thought she could doctor for me."

Vivian rises up a bit on her toes to look, but she doesn't come off the porch.

He laughs again. "Most of Lynn's mutts would bite you worse than me, girly."

"What's wrong with the dog you brought?"

"Ran off on a cougar hunt and found some bait I'd set up in a steel-jaw. Sprung the trigger on her own leg."

"Is it bad?"

"It's not bleeding much anymore, but it's swole up a bit and she won't walk on it."

Vivian glances past him again at the back of his truck.

He says, "Lynn'll be mad if you don't help a customer. Why don't you come on down here? Look things over for me."

"I don't know how to care for injuries."

"Aw, now. You look like you'd make a fine nurse to me."

Vivian takes another step back, pulling open the screen and tripping over the threshold.

"Easy does it," he says. He starts up the steps, and she closes the screen door and latches it.

She says, "I'm going to have to ask you to come back later."

He is on the porch now, looking in at where she stands, just the thin screen between them guarding the threshold.

"Well now," he says grinning. "That might be the nicest invitation I ever got."

He clomps back down the porch steps then and slaps his leg and calls to his dog. "Dizzy!" he says. "Get in, Dizzy girl."

The dog whirls around, and he laughs, looking up at the porch and tipping his hat as he puts it back on and climbs in. Then he drives away fast, spraying gravel.

It is a long time after he disappears out of sight down the highway that Vivian moves from her spot gripping the screen door. She looks over her shoulder into the deep dark of the room where her babies lie sleeping, and then she takes off Lynn's boots and leaves them by the door.

She tries first in the kitchen, throwing open each of the cupboards and drawers, peering in back and shifting bowls and plates to check behind them. The room looks chaotic when she is finished, with all of Lynn's cupboard fronts hanging open and the contents of her own backpack still heaped on the table in a froth of used tissues, and she stands in the center, breathing hard and thinking, before she closes Lynn's cupboards and turns to move on. She can see the stairs from here, and she looks up the steep rise, considering them, but then she passes them up and goes back into the little hall. There is a tiny mail table where Lynn keeps her keys, and it has a drawer in it, but when she pulls it open she finds nothing but chapstick and a deck of playing cards and loose change in a little bowl. She closes it and faces the coat closet. She has to stand on her tiptoes to feel around on the top shelf above the coats and there she finds a wide-brimmed sun hat, a pair of woolen mittens, and a basket of dog leashes. The coats hanging number half a dozen and she reaches into the pocket of each, feeling, coming up with a ziplock bag of almonds in two of them and a handful of dog treats in almost every one.

On the floor behind Lynn's boots Vivian finds the liquor carton. She crouches and pulls it forward, and it is out of surprise at the volume of alcohol more than anything else that she begins opening the flaps to peer in and pull out the bottles. Then it is the mystery of their emptiness that makes her continue, pulling out each one and finding the neck tape broken and the glass empty and clean and then sliding it back down in. After three, she just opens the box lids, one after another, not pulling the bottles out but just glancing at the broken tape, until she reaches the last row and notices no bottle, and reaches down inside to find what's there.

When she draws the pistol out, she holds it at first like a letter she is reading, sideways and two-handed, noting the slight waffle print on the grip, and the circle of steel that guards the trigger, and then it seems to occur to her to check to see if it is loaded, although she is not sure how. She holds it up, eyeing the parts that move—the hammer and the safety, and the magazine catch—still careful to hold it only by the tip of the stock and the tip of the barrel, always keeping the muzzle pointed away from her own body, all the while just crouching there in the hall with her head to the dark closet of coats and boots and her back to the world behind her, and suddenly the gravity of what she is doing, snooping and discovering a kind woman's secrets and the hiding place of a weapon that defends her out here alone, and also too her own first holding of a gun—it builds up on her and makes her whirl her head around, looking over her shoulder and up at the door.

But there is no one there.

She looks down again at the gun. Then she straightens up to standing. She peers into the living room before she goes, seeing just one puppy awake, pulling with a soft ripping sound at a rag in a far corner of the fencing while his siblings sleep, and the mama dog sleeps too, and beyond there Vivian's own babies still make no sound at all.

She unlatches the porch door and steps out, holding the gun low but ready at her side as she had seen Lynn do early that morning facing the shadow of her own car. Then she raises her arm and sights along the sleeve of her borrowed coat. She can see the post in the distance with the cans below it, and she wonders if Lynn stood back here this far, and how good it would be to know you could shoot something you aimed at from this distance. She puts up her other hand now, because her arm is shaking, and she squeezes one eye shut, and she thinks she can see it right there where the barrel points—the series of holes Lynn made in the post when she herself was trying to learn.

Vivian lowers the gun and goes inside, hurrying a bit, and puts the pistol back where she found it. She closes all the box tops, patting them, as if they might pop open on their own, and slides the carton back in. She tips her head this way and that as she arranges and rearranges the boots in front until she is satisfied. She closes the door.

In the kitchen she takes Lynn's breakfast drink out of the refrigerator. It has thickened a bit, into something almost solid. She takes a spoon from the drawer and stirs it. Then she sits down at the table. Her yellow backpack is still open, and her things are still spilled out around it—her wallet with no money in it and the zip purse full of cigarettes she will not smoke until later, outside, because this house is not her own—and she draws the *People* magazine toward her through the sea of tissues and picks up the sparkly pink phone. She skips the first three messages to play the last, sitting perfectly upright as she listens:

"Vivian, this is Carla Bonham calling again. I just want to make sure you understand that calling me back doesn't mean you have to testify. I just want to hear your story. I know it was a long time ago and you might want to leave it there, but what you say could really help a girl who is hurting a lot right now. She's very scared herself to get up there and say what happened, and she asked me to pass along to any girls he might have done the same to that you could change her life by helping her win this trial and also help her make sure this never happens to any other girl again. Whew! That's a mouthful. Sure would be easier to talk voice-to-voice. Call me."

Vivian sets the phone on the scarred wood table. The little rhinestones catch late morning light through the dog yard window. She reads the article about movie-star mothers now. It's just pictures mostly. Pushing their babies in swings and smiling. Or crouching to point at ducks in a park. All of them pretty, and the captions say things like "Uma Plays Mama," and "Jessica Jokes with Jaya." Vivian studies each one before she turns the page. She doesn't read anything else. She closes the magazine and rolls it up and opens the cupboard under the sink where Lynn keeps a garbage can, and she slips it in among the skins of the avocados, and then she takes all her old tissues off Lynn's table, heaping them in on top in three loads, and shuts the cupboard door with almost no sound.

She drinks the smoothie finally, doing it all in one long series of gulps, leaning back. Her eyebrows knit together as she adjusts to the strange flavor. Then she wipes her lips as Lynn did, forefinger and thumb, and she rinses the glass in the sink, and soaps it too, and rinses it again and sets it in the drying rack beside the old woman's.

6

Unpleasant Surprises

It is still dark out when Dana pulls up to the big gate in her white Jetta. She rolls down her window and presses a four-digit code into the keypad on the pole, and the big black iron halves swing open slowly and she eases through, past the white Spanish housefront and through an arch, past the garage bays in back and down a little hill to a small pea-gravel parking area where two black Suburbans are parked beside a little cottage with a terra-cotta tile roof, its shuttered windows bleeding seams of light. Behind her in the car, her dress with the peach-colored flowers hangs inside a clear bag for the wedding. She shuts her engine off.

She shoulders her backpack and steps out, and she looks up at the house. The lower floor is dark, and up above are two bright squares, and then two with the sort of soft blue glow that night-lights make in a room. The rest is dark.

Dana walks the path to the cottage, her feet crunching in the gravel. Crickets chirp and sprinklers hush against the thick green leaves of the camellia bushes that hem it in. She presses her code into a keypad on the wall, and when the door swings open, the room is empty. Just a wall of folding tables laden with computers and monitors partitioned into grainy black-and-white quarter-screen views of the property. On the fourth monitor she can see a blurry figure heading uphill toward the house, and then in another quadrant crossing into view next to the tennis court, and then on screen three opening the door to a shed next to the greenhouse. "Hi, Larry," she hears through a speaker on the table. "Dana just keyed in at the gate. I wanted to go over a few things with you before I check her in." She reaches to turn one of the volume knobs down.

There are still sounds in the small room after she does this. Street noise from one of the speakers: the passage of a car in front of the gate. She can also hear the cricket noise she had heard in the yard, and the hush of the sprinklers, and she leaves these on, setting her backpack on the floor with her eyes on the screens, and sitting down in the empty chair in front of them.

She looks at each quadrant in turn. The long rectangle of a covered swimming pool. A play structure with a tube slide beneath a tree. Hedge lines and fence lines. Street and gate. Tennis court. Greenhouse. And finally a fish-eye view of the front doorstep to the house, four small sneakers lying jumbled beside the mat.

She begins the sequence again: swimming pool, play structure, fence line, hedge line, street, gate, tennis court, greenhouse, door.

The sound of a jogger comes over one of the speakers: heavy steps on pavement; a cough. Only his shadow appears in the screen shot of the gate itself, but then finally he appears on screen two, in the shot of the north approach up the street.

The door opens behind Dana then, and she stands. A bald man in a black knit shirt and tan pants like her own.

"Little change of plan," he says. He sits down in the chair and looks up at her. "Today's detail switching to travel duty. Principal One is taking a road trip to Las Vegas. Length uncertain, but up to two nights likely. I can get backup to drive there and swap with you midday if you can't extend beyond your scheduled shift. If you have another commitment."

Behind Larry on the screens every part of this small personal world they have been asked to monitor for dangers holds still; nothing moves.

The moment between his question and her answer stretches out in Dana's mind, although she does not allow it to last more than a few seconds. Already she has tried out and discarded the private pretense that the urge to say yes is born of professionalism. Dana is not a woman who fools herself. She will say yes because weddings make her uncomfortable anyway; because the news she planned to tell Ian in the chapel parking lot is bad; because she prefers to lose him over the phone, from a motel room. On the floor something inside her heavy backpack settles suddenly, tipping it to rest against her leg.

"Certainly," she says.

"Fantastic." He picks up a stack of tabbed folders from the table behind him. "She's shooting for leaving at six thirty. She wants to drive herself, and she'll be picking up a dog from her father's house in Summerlin and then visiting him at Summerlin Hospital. Velasquez went ahead a few hours ago to do reconnaissance and reserve rooms at a motel that takes dogs. I'd like you to follow her on the drive up."

He holds out one of the folders. "Maps from here to house, house to motel, hospital to motel, motel to hospital."

Dana reaches out to take it.

He says, "Velasquez sketched out an internal map of the hospital. He says they check identification and restrict movement inside, so he scheduled contingency doctor's appointments for both of you."

He hands her two more folders.

Then he picks up a clipboard and takes a pencil from beside his keyboard. "Okay. Protective Asset Inventory. You ready?"

Dana crouches on the linoleum at his feet and unzips her backpack.

He looks down at his checklist. "Current company-issued first-aid kit?"

She withdraws a red zippered pouch and sets it on the linoleum floor.

"Satellite phone?"

She lays one of these on the linoleum as well.

"Flare gun?"

She pulls out a black plastic case.

"Fire starter?"

She takes out a ziplock bag containing a box of waterproof matches and a green disposable lighter.

"Emergency food rations?"

Four vacuum-sealed pouches of silver foil.

"Pepper spray?"

A small orange canister.

"Camera?"

A Nikon D3 and a telephoto-lens case.

"Duty weapon?"

From under the hem of her shirt she withdraws a SIG Sauer 229 9mm pistol and lays this on the floor as well.

"Have you consumed any alcohol in the last twenty-four hours?"

"No, sir." She begins repacking her supplies.

He makes a checkmark. "Have you maintained your contractual commitment to abstain from use of nicotine and recreational drugs?"

"Yes, sir."

"Are you in good health?"

"Yes."

"Any recent fever, unusual fatigue, vomiting, or other signs of illness?"

She looks up at him, one hand on her open backpack. "I vomited twice yesterday, sir."

He looks down at her from his chair.

She says, "I was able to complete my Stress Inoculation Training with an improved score. I don't have any concerns about my ability to accept this detail and perform to my highest standards."

"But what about getting your protectee sick?"

"I won't, sir."

"How can you know that?"

"It's not contagious."

He rocks back in his chair. "How the hell can you possibly know that?"

The room is really no more than a shed's width, so small they are almost touching. "I'm pregnant, sir."

He puts a hand on top of his bald head like a yarmulke.

She says, "It's just morning sickness, and I can control it."

"I'll be damned."

"I felt nauseated before I even put my bite suit on yesterday, and I put on my equipment, completed the test, left the yard, went inside to the bathroom, closed the door, and took off the helmet and suit jacket before I vomited."

"Jesus, Dana." He forces his hand back to the desktop. "I mean, congratulations."

"Thank you. Although I should point out that it's not news I would otherwise share since I don't plan on completing the pregnancy."

"Oh. Well, okay. Let's see." He looks down at his clipboard again. He has lost his place. Over a speaker on the monitoring table they can hear the sound of a door opening and shutting. On the upper right-hand quadrant of screen four a dog streaks by the play structure, and then, a second later, an older dog limps past, and then another second later, a smaller dog with its hindquarters dragging behind on a wheeled platform.

Larry says, "One more on the list: 'Have you experienced any recent emotional challenges that would compromise your concentration on this mission?' "

"No, sir."

"Because I could understand if, um . . . if that kind of decision . . . "

"It doesn't, sir."

"Tony is on backup call this morning. He has his bags here."

"I hope you'll trust me on this."

He scratches his chin.

She says, "If I might be bold here, agents have stressors all the time that they keep private if they feel they're below a certain threshold of distraction. That's what I would have done in this case had it not been for my honesty about the vomiting question."

He purses his lips, considering. Dana lowers her head and continues repacking her backpack, taking care with the things inside. Finally she zips it and stands, lifting the hem of her shirt to holster her gun.

He reaches for a set of keys on a hook on the wall. "This one has a full tank," he says, handing them to her.

"Thank you, sir."

She picks up the briefing folders, the last thing she needs for this journey, and she steps out into the purpling dawn.

The black Suburban is beyond her own car, in the deeper dark of the shade cast by an avocado tree bearing a swing made of a tethered tire. She walks toward it, past her own car with her dress for the wedding hanging in back, past a tricycle and an empty milk crate, past the litter of fallen fruit, to stand in the narrow space between the swing and the door of the car. The swing is little used, it seems, the rope frayed, and inside the circle of black rubber hides something inanimate and invisible save for a pair of white plastic eyes that reflect back the first bit of light clouding in below the tree. Dana does not touch it, but she stares a moment, standing among the fallen avocados, her eyes adjusting, until she makes out the shape: a dark-cloaked action figure holding a sharpened pike.

Dana turns away then, toward the pale shine of chrome keyhole and door handle standing out in the heavy shade. She unlocks it and gets in, closing the door on the noise of sprinkler and crickets, setting her backpack and folders on the seat beside her, and she sits there in the quiet. The clock on the dashboard reads 6:15.

She takes out her phone and opens a text template. She enters Ian's name and types:

> Work detail changed to overnight travel duty. I'm sorry. I know this is really bad for you.

She looks at it a few seconds, the cursor blinking. She looks to her left, not out her window but at it—at the way it curves and the way it meets the door frame. Most people cannot tell, but the glass on the cars their company issues is thicker than normal window glass: bulletproof. She looks back down at her BlackBerry, at her start of a message to Ian. She adds:

> Meanwhile, I have some important news to share so

She backs up and tries again:

> Also, I'll call you during one of my breaks because there's something I should
>
> something I owe it to you to
>
> something I feel obliged

She backs all the way up again and looks at what she has. Just a last-minute regret for the wedding, and an apology for the smaller disappointment she knows this will be.

She presses Send.

She sets her BlackBerry in the cup holder then, and with her remaining time, she makes some preparations. She eats a saltine and takes a sip of water. She lays an empty ziplock bag and a soft-pack of wet wipes on the passenger seat. She takes a small white trash bag from her backpack and sets it up, pinning the long top edge behind the glove-box door. She takes the folders she prepared the night before—"Insurance Claim Denial Appeals" and "Planned Parenthood Clinic Forms"—and moves them to a rear exterior pocket in her backpack to make room for the folders that her shift manager has given her in the front. In the cup holder her phone lights up suddenly. A reply from Ian. Above an excerpt from her own message, "I know this is really bad for you," he has typed this:

> We'll see.

Dana breathes a little puff of surprise through her nose. She sits staring at it for so long that when she checks the clock again she sees that it is time to leave. She sets her BlackBerry back in the cup holder. She puts the key in the ignition and turns. She backs up in the armored Suburban, past her white car with the dress for the wedding still waiting in the backseat, and turns around, pulling forward finally, up to a closed garage door and stops just shy of it so that she is not blocking the threshold.

Jessica stands in the center of a big walk-in closet stuffed full of the things she wears and the things she wants to hide. On the shelves jeans and T-shirts sit stacked among clear plastic bins of sunglasses and baseball caps, and in the corners, on either side of a big mirror she avoids looking in this morning, skirts of evening gowns spill out from behind baskets heaped high with dirty laundry, a big gilt-framed collage Akhil made of her film reviews, and the life-sized cardboard cutout of her in a flight suit that her daughters would not let her throw away. The skylight is dark above her, and she is already dressed in her big sweatshirt and jeans. Her running sneakers are on and tied. She is bending to place an extra baseball cap into an open duffel bag when Akhil appears in the doorway in his T-shirt and striped pajama bottoms, his hair wild with sleep, rubbing his eyes.

"I let the dogs out to pee; they were scratching. Wait—what are you doing?"

"I'm going." She slides open a drawer.

"I thought we talked about this last night. I thought you agreed with me."

She sifts through her socks. "Please don't try to talk me out of it."

She puts a pair of socks in her duffel, and Akhil disappears and appears again quickly with a laptop and a serious, purposeful look on his face. He opens it on top of her dresser. He begins tapping.

She tries to keep packing as he reads. He is not the type to exaggerate his delivery, but his raised eyebrows and his pattern of emphasis betray his disdain. " 'I'm so worried about you, Sweetheart. I care about you so deeply, and I know you well enough to know that you will never love yourself if you let yourself be lured by the spoils of fame into turning your back on your family. You are not the type to be ashamed of your humble beginnings. Perhaps one of the members of your entourage could redo the seating charts and find a little space in the back for me, behind all the stars?' "

Jessica's lip trembles. She bites it and looks at the ceiling in front of her open drawers. "It's such poisonous crap. Such evil manipulative garbage. I don't know why I still let it bother me."

"Because it's poisonous evil manipulative garbage from your own dad," he says.

"I wasn't keeping him away because I was ashamed of him! And there were no stars at our wedding! There was no entourage!"

"Baby, it's me." He smiles sadly and tries to catch her eyes with his own. "I was there, remember?"

She turns back to her drawers. "It doesn't matter. I still want to go." She opens another drawer.

Akhil keeps reading: " 'Because I love you so very deeply and I worry over the moral anguish I know you feel in your heart about having let your fame separate you from your family, I need to share with you the tragic story of my great-aunt Peg, who might have died without bitter regrets if she had only forgiven her father their past misunderstandings and allowed him just once to meet his grandchildren.' "

Jessica grabs a fistful of underwear and stuffs it in the bag at her feet. "You're not changing my mind."

He says, "Or this: 'I'm so confused by your anger, Dearheart. I tried to call and ask your permission but your handlers wouldn't let me speak to you, and it honestly never occurred to me you would say no because it's such common practice among the more compassionate stars. Didn't Angelina sell family photos to *People* to benefit UNICEF? Didn't you say you cared about the plight of children in India?' "

She leans over and zips the bag shut.

He says, "It's a setup, Jessica. You're doing exactly what he wants you to do."

"We can't know that for sure. It wasn't even him calling."

"Who cares? For all we know that woman on the phone was one of the paparazzi friends he splits commissions with. He's a pretty creative guy, remember?" He flips the laptop around: a scanned screen shot from TMZ with a headline that reads, "Father's Day in Beverly Hills: No Dads Allowed" next to a picture of a sparkly-eyed older man smiling for the camera outside the gate in front of their house with a sign that says, JESSICA PLEASE FORGIVE ME!

Akhil says, "They actually have that one posted as a sample on one of the celebrity photo brokering websites with dollar signs stamped across it."

She picks up the duffel by the strap and slings it over her shoulder. "You were right last night, Akhil."

"About what?"

"I have to stop hiding in here. Growing up with a mother who's afraid to go outside or answer the phone is way worse than growing up knowing your grandfather is an asshole."

Akhil's hands shoot up in the air. His eyes are wide with surprise and excitement. "Good! Great! Hallelujah! That's my girl!" Then he lowers them and grabs her gently by the shoulders. "But that means go back to work. That means go outside. That doesn't mean run headlong into one of your dad's ambushes."

"I have to."

"Why?"

"Because." She puts her hands on her hips. "Because I want my dog."

He shakes his head briskly, as if someone slapped him. "Wait, what?"

"I want the dog, Akhil." She folds her arms across her chest. "That's my dog. Grace Kelly. That's one of the dogs he bought for me."

He narrows his brows skeptically. "When you tracked him down at seventeen . . . After he abandoned you as a baby . . ."

"See! I knew you would say that. That's why I didn't tell you last night." She reaches into a basket of sunglasses on top of her dresser and grabs a pair.

He says, "One of the litter of eight puppies he got on impulse for his tenement studio—"

"Yes."

"For you to rush home and feed between your high school classes while he was out sprinkling bits of broken glass into his food at Denny's or slamming on his brakes in front of teenage drivers."

"Yes."

"There is probably no dog at all, Jessica; she should have died years ago; she'd have to be ancient by now—"

"I thought of that! It's possible! I looked it up, even!"

"Or there might be a different dog he paid that woman to call Grace Kelly to lure you out there for a photo ambush. 'Jessica Finally Forgives!' 'Dog and Threat of Deathbed Trump Five-Year Star Grudge!' "

She puts on her cap and glasses. "Maybe." Then she muscles past him into the dark hall with her bag, past the two closed doors and down the narrow stairs into the kitchen. She fills the coffee carafe with water and pours it into the coffeemaker. She scoops coffee into a filter, making a sloppy job of it, while Akhil stands behind her blinking, watching her. Finally she opens the refrigerator and takes out a little ziplock snack bag of leftover bacon.

"Let me make you an egg," he says.

"It's not for me, it's for Grace," she says, and she bends over her duffel bag to stuff it inside. When she stands again, he is closer, and he takes her head gently in his hands. He kisses her on her hair. "All the more reason to make you an egg, then."

Jessica sits down on a stool at the counter, and watches him take a carton of eggs from the refrigerator. He pours a little oil in a pan and turns on the flame beneath it. In the wake of her struggle against them, his bald truths make her feel cared for, every bit as much as the egg. Her father's false comforts had been flawless. Perfect fits. Measured with some bloodless micrometer against the opening of her sorrow and then jiffy-milled—quick-crafted behind his shining eyes, as if turned on a lathe. The egg sputters and pops on the stove, and Akhil watches it while beside him the carafe clouds with steam and finally releases a trickling stream of dark coffee, and then he slides the egg onto a plate, the same kind of flowered dish she had used for the girls the night before. The whole time they were dating, he never once flattered her or sent her too many flowers or told her anything she loved hearing that later turned out to be untrue. Instead he sent an envelope of vitamins to her trailer. He told her he liked the smell of her breath after she ate grapes. Now he takes a fork from the drawer and hands it to her and watches as she cuts into the egg with the side of her fork and takes an enormous bite. A little ghost of red glitter spangles the floor beneath her. The skin around her eyes is puffed and splotched pink from crying.

He says, "At least let me come with you."

She shakes her head.

He says, "I can be dressed in two minutes. It's perfect. I'm not on duty until Wednesday."

"I might not be back by then."

"I'll catch a flight if that happens."

"What about your class for the residents?"

"Not until Thursday."

"But you have all those articles to read! And a recertification exam on Friday!"

"I can prep in the car while you drive."

She opens her mouth to raise another objection, and before she can speak he adds, "And the girls will be fine; my mother is probably already awake in her bed reading John Grisham and munching a bag of Kashmiri mix."

"Okay, you're right." She blinks, looking baffled, or caught, or both. "I guess I just don't want you to come."

"Why on earth not?"

"I want to face him on my own. All these layers of protection!—"

When Akhil opens his mouth to object, she waves her fork impatiently; "I don't mean Security. I've already talked to Larry. He's assigning two people to come with me."

"Then what *do* you mean?"

"You were right about the unread scripts. You were right about me hiding in here for the last four years. But it's not just the house. It's you and the girls I'm hiding behind. You *know* me. I like the version of me you see. It feels so safe. All the lousy distorted things people say—even nice people! Even people who think it's a compliment!—none of it confuses or depresses me when you're with me. I need to learn to do that for myself."

He watches her stand and take a silver travel mug from the cupboard and fill it with coffee. As much as he'd like to go with her, he will not try to argue her on this. She had once laid out a collection of her red-carpet photos from the days before she met him, and although she looked stunning, right away he knew what she was trying to show him. There was a sad, tense look in her shoulders and mouth that was absent in the pictures with him at her side. In the manic strobe-lighting of camera flashes, under the cacophony of pleas ("Over here, Jessica!" "Give us those eyes, Jessica!" "Jessica, tell us who you're wearing!") he'd taken to whispering his own in her ear ("Mommy, cut my crusts!" "Jessica, who did your epic bedhead!"). It's true it would be good for her not to need him.

"You get how bad it could be, though, right? A whole team of photographers with telephoto lenses in his neighbor's yard to watch you with the dog. If there is a dog. His hospital room bugged so he can sell the conversation to *Hard Copy*. If he's in the hospital. Have you called the hospital?"

"No. I don't want to draw a bigger crowd by tipping anyone off that he's getting a visitor. But I do get it. Paparazzi. Unfair headlines. Heartbreaking betrayal. I get it, Akhil, and I want to go anyway." She clips the lid on the cup with a hard snap.

He studies her face. The wet lashes and the pinked skin and the set jaw.

"Okay, but why, though?"

"Why what?"

"Why do you want that dog? If there is a dog."

"I don't know." She shakes her head, looking first at the tree of photos on the wall and then all around the room. The dirty socks and the struggling Chia pet and the bin of broken toys. "Because it's someone from my family I can take care of? Because it's someone from my childhood I can share with the girls? Because it's something he took from me that I can take back from him?"

Akhil reaches out and tucks a lock of hair behind her ear. He smiles. They have been married ten years, and still it fills her with relief to see how he accepts this about her—her fathomless depths of uncertainty. He is the only mirror she can stand to look in. "Okay," he says.

She picks up her duffel bag, and he follows her into the garage then, its walls lined with shelves of baby gear and old clothes and games they've outgrown, things she is almost ready to give away. She moved these items first to bottom shelves and then into boxes in a hall closet and then here, and on any given day they waver and change in her eyes from keepsakes to junk and then back again. Akhil could sort through them in an hour and never regret (never even remember!) any of his choices. He sheds things so easily, and just as easily he decides what to acquire and what to keep. His mother is the same. Every night she cleans out her purse sitting at the kitchen table, discarding, discarding, but on her bureau she still has a ticket stub from a Zubin Mehta concert she went to as a girl. On shopping trips she never holds an item aloft for long minutes, or circles back on it after she has moved on, or decides to return it as soon as she gets home. She knows her heart, just as Akhil knows his. Their keels are so deep. When Jessica expresses envy over this, he shrugs or kisses her ear or smooths her hair. The primer of his early life was simpler than hers, he says; when she sorts out what to trust from a textbook as convoluted as her childhood, she will know it even more deeply. Maybe so, but until then the ease they feel in the world seems like a magic trick to her. When Akhil first brought Jessica home to meet his parents it was for Lakshmi Puja dinner, and she imagined an arctic front of prejudices would chill their introduction (famous girl, not Indian, higher income, no parents for them to include), but instead his mother stepped forth from the throng of cousins and siblings and aunts and uncles in her sari with her arms outstretched. "Can I be the first one to hug you?" Jessica had tried to invent reasons for such an unconditionally warm greeting in her mind (a love of celebrities, deference to Akhil, a cultural custom), but over the next few years she saw his mother say the same to each new girl- or boyfriend one of her children brought home to her. It was that simple. The people her children loved were people she opened her heart to. They were on the list of things to acquire and keep.

Jessica reaches over an old high chair and a stack of LPs and presses a button on the wall. There is a great cracking and whirring sound, and the garage door begins to draw up and back on its track, filling the garage with the soft gray light from outside, and Jessica opens the door of her Suburban to toss her bag on the passenger seat. When she turns back to say good-bye to him, she sees Jaya standing by his side in her pajamas, holding her stuffed dog and wearing her sparkly red shoes.

"Where are you going, Mommy?"

Prisha was wary and sweet-smart even as an infant nursing in her arms, searching Jessica's face for clues, and then along came Jaya, who nursed with her eyes closed and would drift off to sleep in anyone's lap. To hear her ask a question is to learn for the first time that most questions are asked with a certain guarded skepticism of tone, as if evasion is expected in the answer. Jaya's inflections are so cheerful and open they rise like the shoe-store balloon she once tagged and released with glee on their patio, certain it would drift on hospitable winds to the green yard of a Dutch or Ghanaian or Chinese girl just waiting to be her friend.

Jessica says, "To visit someone in the hospital."

"Who?"

Jessica swallows. Behind Jaya, Akhil is watching her—not expecting her to fail; not expecting anything. The way he studies her face never changes. It is the only scrutiny that makes her feel safe.

"Someone I knew when I was a little girl."

"Can I come with you?"

Jessica smiles at her sadly. "No, sweetie."

"Why not?"

"He's sick in a way that's not safe for kids to be around."

Jaya hugs her stuffed dog to her chest. "Is it safe for you, though?"

"Yes." She bends to kiss her on the top of the head, but as she does so the girl herself bends to do something. When she straightens she is barefoot and holding out her red shoes, and tears spring to Jessica's eyes. She laughs and wipes them away. "I don't need those, sweetie."

The girl doesn't lower her arm. "How do you know?"

"It's just a hospital. It's not the kind of place you get stranded."

"You might not know, though. I don't think Dorothy knew."

"Okay," she says. She takes the tiny shoes and sets them on the seat next to her duffel bag. "But don't worry. Tell your older sister I'll be back soon, will you? Tell her I said good-bye."

The girl hugs her dog. "I'll let Daddy tell her."

"Why?"

"She'll tell me something scary. She likes to scare me."

"There's nothing to be scared of."

"Last night she said the witch was Dorothy's neighbor. She said maybe Mrs. Lucas is one and we don't know it yet."

Akhil steps forward and lays his hands on Jaya's shoulders. He winks at Jessica over her head. "Turns out witches aren't as hard as they seem to get rid of, though. She turned back into a neighbor as soon as Dorothy splashed her with water, didn't she? She was Dorothy's to dissolve all along." He leans over Jaya's head to kiss Jessica on the cheek. He whispers, "Call me. I'll call you if you don't. I still think it's crazy not to take an ally."

Jessica gives a little nod toward Dana's Suburban idling quietly just shy of the threshold. "I'm taking her, aren't I?"

"Yes. And thank you. But that's not the only kind of safe I want you to be."

He pulls away and lets her go then, shutting the door gently and stepping back as she slowly backs out, looking at her with sad eyes but waving cheerfully until she turns, her rear bumper lining up with Dana's, and they pull out together, picking a path among the tricycles and the balls, over the chalk drawings, all of them more brightly colored now with the first direct sun, and as the big gate halves swing open, Jessica glances at her rearview mirror for one last look at them behind her. Then she drives out through her gate into the street to begin her journey, fitfully at first, with traffic lights making her pause and watch strangers pass, until she crosses up over the green hills and down onto the long stretch of highway through Death Valley, dry and silent on either side of her for miles, with Jaya's small red shoes sparkling on the passenger seat next to her, and Dana following behind.

After hours of parched flat desert, they come up over another small mountain pass, and Las Vegas appears in the distance, a weird emerald expanse of golf greens around a center of glittering buildings thrown up to look like the rest of the world's wonders—marvels other cities shaped with time and trial. The last stretch of gray highway bears them around a bend over the barren sands and dumps them abruptly into that uncanny green valley, and Jessica follows her map to Villa Ridge, a wide curving clean street of lovely stucco houses, all of them with high arched windows and sparkling lanterns above their front doors. A palm tree sprouts from each jewel green front lawn, except for the last, where a yellow skid loader sits parked on a plot of fresh soil next to a giant hole and a small fan palm, its root-ball wrapped in burlap. Even with her car windows closed, Jessica can hear the barking.

She pulls up in front of it and turns her engine off. She reaches over Jaya's red shoes for the bag of bacon in her duffel, and feels an upwelling of a familiar dread, not at the prospect of entering her father's yard, or of being photographed by waiting strangers, but of something more immediate and more common—her smallest, most ridiculous fear—of greeting Dana. She suppresses it certainly (she is grateful every day for the protection they provide from the shadows her job has cast on her family—the predatory photographers, the stalkers, the few famous kidnappings of children of stars), but the truth is she does not go whole days or even whole hours at home without wondering what these kind people think of her. It's embarrassing. It seems to her the pinnacle of vanity and self-absorption, this discomfort she feels around people who are paid to protect her privacy, people who in reality are probably bored by her. It is bad enough that she allows herself to be buffeted by magazines' misleading snapshots and captions (Sex Symbol! Rich Bitch! Super Mom! Selfish! Icon! Bad Daughter!), but secretly she finds herself feeling insecure and self-conscious even in her own yard, where from behind a shuttered window she knows good people can see her. She has made her world so small trying to escape the judgments of strangers, drawing in and in, shopping online and hosting events, until she rarely leaves home, and they are the only strangers left to fear. And she finds that for her they are plenty. They, after all, have more pictures to piece together, and although of course all they see her doing is collecting sippy cups and pushing her girls on a swing, she finds herself haunted by a mystical idea of the composite they see on those four quarter screens—as if (crazy! she knows it!) they see more than she herself can, some kind of objective collage, a magical slide show of her life's most telling details, a window to her past, herself, her soul.

She looks in the rearview mirror to adjust her cap and glasses and sees that Dana is already getting out of her Suburban and approaching, a tall thin woman with a blank pale face, khaki pants neatly pressed and her black polo shirt loose, hanging low over her belt to hide a gun.

She arrives at Jessica's window. The scar on her upper lip is a bright spot in her face, which is so neutral it makes Jessica first nervous, and then ashamed in exactly the way she expected to be. She rolls her window down, resolving not to do it this time. She will not try to influence this woman's opinion. She will not work to project what she wants others to see (Kind! Down-to-earth! Humble! Normal!). But even as she does so, she finds herself saying, "Thanks for coming on this trip. Dana, right?"

"Yes, ma'am."

"Larry said really great things about you."

"That's nice to hear, ma'am."

"Jessica."

Dana just smiles. Jessica has to cut her eyes away for a moment, because of the frankness of Dana's scrutiny, and because of the revealing strangeness of what she is working up to ask. "Anyway, thank you, really. I appreciate the help," she says. Then into the long opening of her nervous hesitation Dana interjects:

"I think I should lead you around the corner, to park farther from the house."

Jessica blushes and glances at her father's raw yard, as if Dana has divined something about her just from looking at it. The dog's barks are sharp and evenly spaced, as if they too are measuring something.

"We'll attract less attention if the cars are not together," Dana explains. "I thought I'd keep mine closer, in case we have to leave quickly."

And the relief Jessica feels at this practical explanation shames her all over again.

"I'll show you where," Dana says, and jogs ahead of her. Jessica drives slowly, following the figure of her, this slim woman running along the sidewalk and around the bend to where more clean houses lie. The barking there is just as loud. It could be the same street, but for the missing spectacle of her father's unfinished yard. She adjusts her cap and sunglasses again. She stuffs the bag of bacon into the patch pocket on her sweatshirt and looks at the shoes her daughter gave her. She gets out of the car.

Dana stands, waiting.

Jessica clears her throat. Although her own eyes shift toward the corner with every bark, Dana's hold steady, watching her. In Larry's travel-support summary, Jessica saw that in high school Dana was a decorated member of the Marine Corps Junior ROTC. That she speaks Arabic and served four years in the barren and bloody deserts of Afghanistan and Iraq. What must she be thinking? And when will she, Jessica, ever, *ever* stop wondering what people are thinking? It is an advantage only in character acting, to indulge so compulsively in speculation about the private thoughts of other people. She closes her eyes briefly and pictures her two daughters on the swing set in her backyard. *I am just a mother. I am just a mother who loves, like all mothers, to watch her girls swing.* But she knows Dana is staring at her, waiting. No doubt wondering why she is so nervous around a woman whose job it is to keep her safe. Ridiculous. It's ridiculous, this beating around the bush. Jessica tries again: "I need to ask you for something."

"Certainly."

"So I guess you know all about my dad. Read about him online or seen him on TV or—"

"Larry briefed me this morning, ma'am."

Jessica's eyes cut off to the side and flutter uncomfortably. She crosses her arms and forces herself to look back at Dana's eyes. This woman will not understand it, what she wants to ask for. Even Jessica does not understand it.

She says, "So I don't really know what to expect here. I mean, I don't know who might be waiting—"

"There's currently no one in the yard with the dog, and the house itself is still empty to the best of our knowledge."

Jessica's forehead wrinkles in confusion.

"Velasquez did a pretext visit," Dana says. "He left for the hospital just a minute before we pulled in."

"He rang my dad's doorbell?"

"Yes, ma'am."

"Who was he pretending to be?"

"A census taker."

Jessica longs to be more like them. That is part of it, she remembers now—part of her shame around them. It's not just physical danger they're willing to face bravely—it's everyday decision. It's logistics and interpersonal nuance. Things are complicated; they're imperfect; and they deal with it. They don't lament and stall. They don't get paralyzed or rush forward in a fog of generalized anxiety and confusion. They assess and act, breaking up a heterogeneous mass of problems into discrete chunks and pairing up often regrettable ends with the best of available means. It seems impossible that they wouldn't be able to call upon these well-honed skills in the daily complexity of their own personal lives. Were she to undertake to play Dana in a film—say, a Dana with a con-man father and a beloved childhood dog condemned to impoundment—she would prep by making a list. She would method-act a set of specific goals and clear desires. She can't imagine they would any of them set off on a journey without knowing what they wanted to find.

The dog is still barking. On either side of them, house upon identical house is lined up impersonally in either direction. Jessica can see that along the hairline of Dana's close-cropped hair there is moisture, but her face is placid, utterly calm.

Jessica says, "So, okay. That's good, then. Um . . . so what I wanted to ask you is . . . to the extent possible, at least . . . just on this trip I'd like to . . . Well, for starters with the dog, I mean, I'd sort of appreciate it if . . . " Jessica is astonished and jealous and annoyed all at once that Dana's face is so unreadable. It seems a feat of strength to betray so little emotion. She presses on, "I mean even if things change, even if photographers show up or are already waiting in the neighbor's house or yard, I'd prefer to be alone. When I go back there to get the dog. Without you, I mean. Even if it means they get a better shot of me going into the yard."

"Certainly. I'll wait right by my car," she says, and she stands there unmoving. Her eyes flick to the right and then to the left and then settle on Jessica again.

"Thank you," Jessica says, still unsatisfied, as if she had hoped her own motives might be revealed to her by Dana's reaction. What is she expecting to encounter in her father's yard? Why is she so desperate to face it so completely alone? But Dana has revealed nothing, and Jessica realizes that the moment has come. There are no tasks that stand between her and what she has come all this way for, whatever that turns out to be.

She sets off for the corner and Dana lags behind her, just as she asked her to, and as she rounds the bend, there in the otherwise unbroken stretch of perfect houses is her father's—pink stucco with a beveled bay window like the others, but marked by the oddly foreboding moat of churned brown soil. Frozen half-submerged in its surface, like sacrifices or weapons borne by visitors who have come before them, are the palm sapling in burlap and the skid loader listing to one side. Jessica pauses on the sidewalk. Then she takes a step, and her father's yard receives her sneaker like the ashy surface of the moon. There is a brown wood gate to the left of the house, a break in the pink stucco wall that separates her from the backyard. It gets larger as she crosses, as do his windows. When she is within grasping distance of the latch something occurs to her. She hesitates and takes a step to the side to peer in through the glass.

What is she hoping for? Perhaps a bit of magic—the flash of insight that comes with a peek into a crystal ball—but what she sees instead is first her own reflection, so familiar and unwanted it chafes at her. She blocks it out impatiently, cupping her hands on either side of her eyes against the glass, but what this reveals is a space almost like a motel room in its impenetrable anonymity. Beige couch. Brown coffee table. Wing chair. Neither shoddy nor expensive. Even the houseplant by the door a minor mystery. It could be a sign he has tended something in the years he has misused her, but just as easily it could be fake. She cannot tell from this distance, and she will never know.

In the wake of each of his mercenary stunts, she had been first outraged and then reflective, finally obsessive. Sleepy-haired over coffee, sautéing onions at the stove, lying in bed with a hand clapped over her eyes, she interjected into the easy marital silence a long memory of her eighteen months living with her dad, stirring the details, sifting them like sand for some clue. Akhil was always patient, listening and watching her with his kind eyes, not even speaking, but she knew what this meant. She responded as if he'd spoken. "Really?" she said. "He'd be off your list? You'd stay away from him? No racquetball or coffee date for him? I thought you said I'd be happier if I accepted my family for what they were."

"I did, and I meant it," he said mildly. "But that means you stop trying to make them into something they're not. You don't attach your happiness to their changing."

"So that means hating him?"

"No, it means not hating yourself for not being able to change him."

"Okay, fine but—" she said, still lost, still none the wiser; how could something that was so clear to him be so opaque for her? "But why can't I be with him and not try to change him?"

"Because he's a grizzly bear of a man. A bumblebee. You don't hate them for what they are, but you keep your distance."

Grace barks again, and Jessica steps away from the window and unlatches the gate to face the scene of her journey's first trial: an empty swimming pool, like a tomb, surrounded on all sides by more churned brown soil, and at the far side a dirty white dog tethered by a chain to a pallet of paving stones. Nearby in the dirt is a mound of dry kibble spilling from a torn-open twenty-pound bag and an orange bucket that says HOME DEPOT across the side. A green hose snakes over the stucco wall and into the bucket from the next yard. The neighbors' walls on all sides are buttressed by a row of high trees—dense Leyland cypress, almost a hedge of it—to block the view of this ragged yard, and although there is no way for Jessica to be certain of it, it is the case that there is no one hiding in among the needled branches. She has what she asked for. She is truly alone.

She lets the gate click shut behind her. Grace doesn't look toward her or change in her pattern of barking as she approaches. Jessica's footing in this soil is unreliable, and she has to wheel her arms for balance and the chasm of the dry white pool looms, tipping and rising in her peripheral vision as she draws near, watching the dog bark, and bark, and bark, at her father's vacant house. Even when Jessica reaches her, stopping five feet from where she has stationed herself, straining at the end of her tether, the dog seems not to see her, and Jessica sees that the whites of her eyes are clouded over like the skins of steamed dumplings. Jessica waves her arms. She claps her hands. Nothing. At last she breaks the ziplock and pulls out a piece of bacon, and as she crushes it in the palm of her hand, the dog finally flinches. She begins to growl.

There is a quick release on the chain attached to her collar. Grace's eyes are unfocused on a point in the sky to the right of Jessica, and her black lips are curled back showing an ugly row of teeth and speckled gums. Jessica takes another step forward, just three feet now from the dog at the end of her tether, and she tosses a few bits of the bacon into the dirt at the dog's feet. Grace stops growling and snuffles for it, biting up a mouthful of soil with each scrap, chewing and swallowing sloppily and then sniffing the air again. Jessica takes another step forward and holds out the last slice, her hand trembling. Grace sniffs the air, and then, so suddenly she has no time to withdraw, lashes out and nips her hard on the hand. Jessica stumbles backward and looks down. Two little puncture marks, the blood welling. She covers it with the cuff of her sweatshirt and looks with astonishment at the old dog who is growling and looking right through her with cloudy eyes.

"I'm right behind you," a voice says.

Jessica turns. There in the dark churned soil, a heavy pack on her back, is Dana.

She says, "Do you know if she's current on her shots?"

Jessica looks down at the puncture marks. The skin around them is beginning to swell and darken. She shakes her head. "I think I surprised her. She seems deaf and blind now."

"Were you trying to feed her?"

"Yes."

"Good. A reason to bite besides rabidity, I mean. Rabies is really rare around here anyway, but it's worth considering."

Dana crouches in the dirt and opens her giant backpack and finds it full of things Jessica needs. She takes out a half-liter bottle of spring water and what seems to be a white matchbook, which she thumbs open to reveal the kind of tiny sewing kit they give away at hotels. She takes out a needle and punctures the top of the bottle.

The dog is still growling.

"What are you doing?" Jessica says.

"I'd like to irrigate it quickly. To reduce the chance of infection."

Jessica pushes up her sweatshirt sleeve and gives Dana her hand. Dana grips her fingers gently as she squeezes the bottle, projecting a fine jet of water at the bite marks. She holds their joined hands low to keep the splash from spraying them in the face, and Jessica steals a glance at Dana's eyes and mouth, which have that same inscrutable look she wore when Jessica told her she wanted to approach the dog without protection, and Jessica knows that Dana is thinking something about what has occurred, she does have an opinion, and even so she is washing Jessica's hand. She looks back down at them where they are joined together.

When the bottle is empty Dana sets it back in her backpack and swabs Jessica's hand with a clean piece of gauze.

"I'll drive you to the hospital," she says.

"No," Jessica says. "I mean—wait." Her hand is throbbing a bit, and it is puffy and blue, and Dana is inches from her, holding it, seeing it tremble and swell. Although at home she might have received all the help she needed through the filter of Dana's black-and-white quarter-screen views, here now in her father's yard there is no choice but to expose herself fully. The object of her dread has taken shape. This is what she was trying to avoid by making Dana wait on the curb.

"I mean, I'm not sure I'm ready. To visit my dad. I might want to wait a bit. Not for anything specific, even, I'm sorry, but I can't even tell you how long it might be."

"To the Emergency Room, I meant." She points to Jessica's hand. "You should get that examined. Tested for nerve damage. Evaluated for rabies prophylaxis."

Jessica feels lightheaded. Something else is bubbling up inside her.

Another layer of embarrassing secret longing revealing itself to her. Something more she'll have to share.

Dana is sealing the used gauze in a clean ziplock. She tucks it into her pack.

Jessica says, "But what about Grace?"

"She's tied up pretty well."

"But Animal Control is coming."

"I doubt anyone else will come back here and get hurt before they can get here."

"No—" Jessica says. The dog barks again, higher and sharper. Jessica's uninjured hand floats trembling to her forehead. She says, "I'm worried they won't try to find a home for her."

Dana stands. "Probably not. Not with a bite history."

"I'm worried they'll just put her down."

"They use pentobarbital. It's an anesthetic, so it puts them to sleep before it kills them. It's totally painless."

"But I want to take her."

Dana switches gears seamlessly. "Certainly. I'm pretty sure they allow owners to observe when they do it, and I'd be happy to discuss that with them for you, but it would be safer to have them transport her and then meet them there."

"No, I mean—" Jessica has no choice but to say it. "I mean I want to take her home with me. I want to try to keep her."

Dana blinks, and Jessica sees that finally she has done it. She has done exactly what she feared. She has given Dana a full peek into her deep well of irrational, emotional, tortured, contradictory, past- and future-bound secret needs. And Dana is shocked. It is the longest Jessica has seen her pause for anything. She begins to believe Dana is stuck; that she has finally frozen her by giving her a set of irrational ends with unimaginable means—a Sophie's choice of her two prime directives, assist and protect. Even for Jessica they are contradictory—Would she bring this angry dog home to her daughters? What is it that she wants?—

but there it is. She knows only that she does not want to leave the dog behind, and she has let Dana see this. She has shown her this bit of insanity. Perhaps Dana will stand here in her father's unfinished yard forever; perhaps her head will explode.

But suddenly Dana nods and says, "I can help you with that," and takes off at a jog across the spongy yard, holding her cell phone up to her ear.

Jessica cannot imagine what she will do. She has left her backpack behind, and Jessica eyes it now lying in the dirt. Its top is open, and inside it Jessica can see a roll of duct tape, a set of tiny screwdrivers, the tops of half a dozen ziplock bags—so simple; so capable; Jessica envies her her bag of separately bagged tools. Her hand is throbbing a bit under the cuff of her sweatshirt, and she feels hot, but the feeling is not unfamiliar to her. She thinks it could be the bite, but just as easily it could be shame. Over expecting the dog to greet her. Over having a father who leaves a dog to rely on the charity and self-preservation instincts of peace- and sleep-starved neighbors. Over getting caught injured by her own needs in her father's yard. It has somehow also to do with being famous, as if instead of a professional accident this too were a choice, and a laughably arrogant and shortsighted one, given how uncomfortable it has made her.

Grace lies down suddenly in the dirt. The hair on her muzzle is a different white, almost gray, and her heavy breath troubles the dry layer of soil, scattering it, setting it rolling. Jessica can hear a car door chuck open and shut, and Dana returns, carrying—what on earth?—a rubber-backed carpet mat from the floor of her Suburban.

She reaches into her backpack and withdraws a roll of duct tape. She wraps the mat around her left arm. She says, "Can you hold this in place a second?"

Jessica is astonished by how relieved she feels to be given such a simple instruction, to have something so physical and uncomplicated to do. She pinches it shut with her left hand while Dana tears off a strip of duct tape. They make an awkward job of it, both of them one-handed, but they manage to tape the mat tight around Dana's arm.

Dana reaches into her backpack again and takes out a ziplock bag of neon green zip ties—extra large, for baling bundles of cable or pipe. "Do you still have some mobility in your right hand? Does it feel okay when you open and close it?"

Jessica clamps her fingers open and closed. "Yes."

"Okay. Here's what I want you to do. I'm going to feed her my left arm, and when she bites down, I'm going to grab her muzzle with my other hand. When I tell you I have full control of her mouth, I'm going to ask you to step in with the cable ties."

She hands the bag to Jessica and takes a step forward. Grace stays where she lies, and for a moment it seems Dana might be able to grab her muzzle with a bare hand before the dog even notices her, but when she draws close enough to reach out, Grace springs to her feet. Dana thrusts out the wrapped arm, and Grace strikes it with her teeth, bouncing once before sinking them into the car mat so hard it buckles. Dana is quick, pinning her muzzle with her free hand and then wrenching her padded arm to get a second hand free and encircle the snout completely. Grace thrashes and Dana straddles her hindquarters and sits on her, bringing her down hard in the dirt. Her turds lie all around them. The dog's breath is loud and wet through her nose. She growls once between Dana's tight-closed hands.

"Ready?" Dana says.

Jessica winces.

Dana says, "Put one of those zip ties right between my two hands."

"But how will she drink?"

Grace scrabbles her paws under Dana's weight, straining to stand, but she doesn't get very far. "Easy, girl," Dana says. To Jessica she says, "I called Velasquez and asked him to meet me at the hospital with a basket muzzle, and then we'll clip off the ties. They can drink through a basket muzzle."

Jessica is still wincing. "Won't it be hard not to cut her?"

"Once we've got the basket on, I can reach through the holes and peel her lips back easily. You'll see."

"Okay," Jessica says. She holds a cable tie limply between her two hands. The blood on her hand is smeared, just tinting the puffy wound pink. "Okay." She steps forward and fits it around the dog's snout, slipping the tip through the eye and then tightening it with a slow, heartbreaking series of clicks.

"Tighter," Dana says.

"But how will you cut it then?"

"I can peel her lips back. It will be easy, I promise. But if you don't do it tighter, she'll push it right off with her paws."

Jessica pulls it tighter.

Dana removes one of her hands. "Let's do a few more."

Jessica winces as she tightens each one. She has to do four before Dana finally lets go of the snout. Right away the dog buries her nose in the soil and scrapes at the ties with her paws, just as Dana said she would, puffing loudly. The two women stand watching, Dana with her hands on her hips and Jessica covering her wounded hand with her sleeve. When it becomes clear she cannot remove them, Grace lies down and whimpers. Jessica's lip trembles, and she bites it to hold back tears. She has always been a sensitive woman, prone to unseemly swells of feeling and tearful sentimentality, and while it has made her a good character actress, Jessica knows, it has also made her quite easy for her father to con. The lip biting doesn't help though. It rarely does. The tears fall and Dana sees them. Jessica begins to cry a little harder; she can't help it. There are more tears, and there is snot she wipes with an ugly sound, and Dana can see and hear all of it standing there beside her, and still nothing changes in the yard.

Then Dana walks past her, past the dog, to the pallet of pavers where the dog's chain is tethered, and, like a character from mythology, Dana lifts a stone to free it. She drags the chain behind her and comes forward to take the dog by her collar and lead her. When Grace tries to stand she struggles a bit, making clear her age and the pain in her joints, but she does not pull away from Dana at all, or thrash. She follows meekly, with her head bowed now, and so does Jessica, staring up at her father's house behind Dana and the dog.

When she nears the gate Dana stops short. "Wait here. I'll go out ahead to check the area and get her secured in the car."

Jessica does as she's told. She hangs back in the shade of the pink stucco wall while Dana unlatches the gate and passes through it with the dog, out across the raw soil to the curb, where a compact elderly woman in a gold velour warm-up suit stands next to a teenage girl in cutoff shorts and a halter top. The girl pulls a purple cell phone from her back pocket and raises it up in front of her face at arm's length between her and Dana. Dana turns her back and walks toward her car.

"Well, wait," the old woman says, walking after her. "Who are you?"

"Just here for the dog, ma'am."

"Are you with Animal Control? That is a famous woman's dog, I'll have you know, and she is on her way here to take care of it. You could have yourself in a spot of very bad PR. DeeDee, are you getting all this?"

"Dang. Hang on a minute. I didn't know there would be anything YouTubeable."

Dana is already across the street. She opens her tailgate and, with unbelievable briskness, slides the makeshift bite sleeve off her arm, hoists the old dog up onto the deck, lowers the door shut with a click, and locks it with the remote in her pocket. The girl scurries across the street and holds the little cell phone up to the window, but with the dark tinting and the reflected light the little screen on her phone shows nothing.

"Burn! Do you think she'll still come, Lulu?"

"Of course she will!"

"I had Mindy and Paco and them coming for pictures and autographs. Mindy made three hundred dollars last year on eBay, and Paco's got a photo credit on Gawker."

The old woman turns to Dana. "Won't you wait a few minutes?"

"I'm afraid that's not possible, ma'am."

"I think it's very unprofessional of you not to wait. She had to drive all the way from Los Angeles, you know. She's going to be just sick over this, she is a very conscientious woman and her father is ill in the hospital. She doesn't have time to be chasing that dog all over creation."

"My apologies, ma'am."

"Let's go inside, DeeDee. We'll call her right now on her cell phone. We can offer to meet her at the hospital."

She puts a hand at the small of the girl's back and ushers her across the raw front yard, right by the gate behind which Dana instructed Jessica to stand waiting. Dana hears the big mahogany door open and shut. Jessica hears it too. As soon as it latches, the brown gate opens and she hurries out and down one block to her own car, parked at an inconspicuous distance where Dana knew from experience to leave it.

On the way to the hospital, Dana leads. Grace is whimpering in the back of her Suburban—a high, rhythmic whine like a squeaky pump—but Dana keeps her eyes on the road, and on her rearview mirror, where she can see Jessica at the wheel of the Suburban behind her. When the hospital rises into view, Dana swings in at the far end of the lot near the Emergency Room portico, past Velasquez nodding Jessica into a parking spot he has waiting for her, and Dana continues on alone, slowing as she passes the benches at the big front entrance, where a young man with mutton-chop sideburns and low-hanging jeans cranes his neck and visors his eyes to see her, a tripod hidden clumsily in the azalea bushes behind him.

She parks at a distance between a silver minivan and a dark maroon Cadillac. She leaves the engine idling, getting out and making a show of looking at him before she crouches out of his sight line to find that Velasquez has done exactly as she instructed. Behind the left front tire of the minivan is a Petco bag, and inside it are two stainless-steel bowls, a bag of chicken-flavored treats, a black plastic muzzle with a leather strap, a nylon leash, and a plastic card key for the Holiday Inn Express with "Rm 105, North Entry" written in black marker above the magnetic strip. It is one of the things that Dana loves about her job—that her coworkers are by requirement predisposed to reliability, to procedure and preparation.

She is still relishing these assets when Grace gives her the first hint that with her they may be useless. When Dana gets back in her car, the dog does not stop whining. Not after Dana climbs over the seats and opens the pouch of treats. Not after she fits the muzzle gently over her nose and clips the cable ties with a pair of blunt-tipped bandaging scissors she brings up from some unknown recess in the backpack from Ian's dreams. Not after she fills a bowl with water from her cooler and sets it down in front of her, splashing a bit to make her take notice. Dana dribbles a bit through her muzzle with a cupped hand and even then Grace holds still, whining, holding her head at a dispirited cant.

It's all she has time for. Dana glances out the back window and sees Jessica and Velasquez pass into the far end of the building while the boy with the camera sits on the stone bench by the door, his eyes fixed on her own car instead. This portion of the mission, at least, will go exactly as she plans. She drops a treat on the surface of the water bowl, hoping the scent might draw the dog's attention later, and she begins unbuttoning her black shirt, leaning forward to remove it. She has to stretch her arms out behind her to do it, and when she wiggles out of it, she reveals a black tank top beneath, a military tattoo on her left bicep, and a pair of shiny aluminum dog tags on a stainless-steel chain. She removes her hip holster, slides up the leg on her khaki pants, slips the gun into an ankle holster on her boot, and pushes the pants back down. She opens an outer pocket on her backpack. Between a bag of cable ties and a clear film canister of safety pins is a cheap pink plastic travel soap case which she snaps open to reveal a selection of lipsticks. She checks the stickers on the bottom and finally uncaps a blackish color and cranks the rearview mirror toward her to put it on. Then she repacks her backpack, cracks all of her windows an inch, and switches her engine off.

The boy sees her coming from a long way off, of course. He squints, shading his eyes under a purple-and-yellow Lakers cap turned sideways. Dana walks differently now, with more sway in her hips, and when she gets close, she sits on the bench opposite without even looking at him and takes a pack of cigarettes out of a side pocket of her backpack. All the while she can see out of her peripheral vision that he is watching her closely. Dana lights her cigarette and takes a drag, blowing it out to the side between her dark lips. Then she unzips her backpack and leans over, moving things around inside, her dog tags jingling, and draws out the camera. It has a wide canvas strap, and she slings it around her neck.

The boy raises his eyebrows. "Who you here for?"

"My grandmother," she says.

The boy snorts.

Dana sets her cigarette on the concrete bench and makes a few adjustments to her camera settings, sighting through the lens at the automatic doors before letting it rest again in her lap on the concrete bench. She leans over her backpack and takes out a small padded zip bag with a different lens in it and removes it from its case. She twists the old lens with a series of tidy clicks, like a soldier disassembling a rifle, and she swaps it out for the longer lens and re-sights on the door.

All the while the kid in the baggy jeans is watching her.

"How long you been doing this?" he says.

Dana says nothing. Instead she picks up her cigarette and takes another drag. Then she takes her BlackBerry out of her backpack.

"Ooh, that's cold," the kid says.

Dana thumbs the keys. Nothing yet from Velasquez. Nothing work-related at all, in fact, but the boy is watching her, and Dana needs him to believe she is corresponding with someone who knows more than he does. So she opens Ian's text.

And above his "We'll see," she types:

> Please provide examples of the lucky turns of fate that might flow from my standing you up at your sister's wedding.

Right away he texts back:

> Didn't you say motel rooms are magical for you? Maybe you'll come home full of pent-up energy from two excellent nights' sleep and need to burn it off.

She smiles.

It works perfectly. "Good tip?" the boy says.

Again Dana ignores him, staring at her screen.

"Your loss," the boy says. He takes out his own cell phone. "I got a girl tipping me about an A-lister." He makes a show of leaning over to check his texts. "I thought we could help each other out."

Dana hits Reply again, but already the burst of pleasure that comes from any communication from him has been replaced by a familiar ache.

She types:

> I'll try to call you on one of my breaks because there's something I need to tell you.

For a long time the ache has been born of something abstract—just that sense from experience that she cannot long hold on to anyone who gets to know her well enough to be disappointed—to discover that there is not more inside her, something she is holding back, some source of warmth or freedom they can uncover or thaw. More recently it has also flowed from something more concrete but still unscheduled—his death, which could be so much sooner than most; it could be anytime; it could be tomorrow. But the ache seems to be taking its final shape now. The object of her dread is more immediate. Dana can see now exactly how she will lose him. She even knows some of the words that will be spoken. And she knows when. It makes her want to hurry. It gives her project a deadline.

She opens the file she e-mailed to herself from her apartment the night before.

Before you appeal, you may want to take some additional steps:

Dana reads through the bullet-pointed recommendations. She reads them twice, even a third time for good measure, still fingering the dog tags between her breasts and taking drags from her cigarette, drawing the boy's attention. She can do this in her sleep—better than she can sleep in fact—all these careful, planful, protective acts. She can perform them for Jessica and for Ian at the same time. Two at once. It is that easy. She has packed into her backpack and BlackBerry and heart everything she needs for an endless stream of defensive feats. Here outside the hospital Dana has disguised herself to appear like the boy—callous, cavalier, shortsighted, mercenary—and although Dana is none of these things, it appears to be working. He is watching her and trying to match her, adjusting his camera settings and eyeing the door and checking his own phone. He cannot know what Dana herself is really reading. He cannot know that Dana is preparing not to unleash pain but instead to try to contain it.

She is on her fifth Sample Letter of Appeal when a text tumbles forth—not from Velasquez (not yet), but from Ian:

Is it yes?

And she is confused for a moment. As he knew she would be, apparently, because before she can parse it, or hit Reply to ask, he sends a second text:

On the after-motel nooky, I mean.

She smiles again, but she forces herself to hesitate this time, because above all Dana is careful. She watches the cursor blink, and knows that somewhere, probably in his breezy, messy, bird-filled apartment, he is waiting to know how she will answer. The answer that had welled up inside her was "We'll see," but she believes (Dana knows) it is not the right thing to say. It is not right because it will mislead him about her plans. The plans she will follow when she is off duty and can call him to tell him the truth about what's inside her. She cannot type, "We'll see," because she will not see. Dana never waits to see. Dana decides and prepares. She decides and prepares based on what she already knows.

So there on the bench in front of the hospital, Dana shifts the big camera between her legs and blows smoke toward the boy, and she tests and weighs, experiments and edits, typing out sterile, cautious phrasing after sterile, cautious phrasing—"Maybe" and "Let's talk first" and "I'm not sure"—until finally she settles on this:

I should leave that up to you after we talk.

And Ian of course does not hesitate. As soon as she sends it, he answers back:

Yes then. If it's up to me it's always yes.

7

Secrets

Lynn parks her truck angle-in in front of the shelter in Winslow. It is a little low concrete building at the end of Main Street—just a long block of storefronts (barber, cleaner, diner) with a school at one end and a church across the street here at the other. She turns her engine off and sits there, looking at the sign to the left of the door: WINSLOW HUMANE SOCIETY. In her rearview mirror is the little reflected image of the church—a dirty white beadboard chapel on a plot of bare dirt. Someone has laid stones in the dirt for a path to its door, and to the left is a rusty swing set—two pairs of chains bearing white plastic seats and the third pair bearing nothing.

She gets out of her car and crosses the wide street toward the chapel—there are no cars passing to stop her—and heads not for the door but for the side of the building, the one facing out of town, where there is a metal handrail surrounding a cut in the earth with a set of concrete stairs leading down.

Lynn slips her hands into the big patch pockets of her barn coat. Then she takes the stairs down to a little wood door with a dented metal knob and she pushes it in and open.

The room is small, lit by a metal floor lamp and the light from a high slit of a basement window, and in the center is a circle made by seven chairs and a plywood podium. In four of the chairs sit men and at the podium stands a woman (younger than Lynn) taking a sip of water from a clear plastic cup. More chairs sit folded up against the wall at the back. All the faces turn to her when she opens the door.

The woman with the cup of water clears her throat. "Welcome," she says.

Lynn steps in and sits down.

The men turn back to look at the woman at the podium. She takes a sip of water, her throat making a little squirting noise as she swallows and sets the plastic cup on the plywood with a hollow, skittery sound.

"My name is Beth," she says, "and I'm an alcoholic."

Over the pulse in her ears, Lynn hears her tell a story of how she used to bake cookies with her six-year-old daughter. Beth does not look at her directly, but she can tell somehow that this is not the story Beth had planned to tell. It ends with Beth passing out and her daughter, who now lives with her ex-husband's parents in Arizona, trying to take the burning cookies from the oven herself.

She sits down and smooths her wide sprigged skirt with her palms.

The men shift in their seats. One of them, a man in work boots and denim overalls with a white handlebar mustache, clears his throat. "I came to thirty-seven meetings before I said a single blessed word to anyone."

Another, a handsome young Hispanic man in jeans and big white sneakers says, "That's right, Vernon, you did."

Vernon gives his knees a squeeze with his ruddy hands.

Looking at the floor between their feet, Beth says, "We're glad you came again."

The remaining two men are an elderly black man wearing a belt and polished shoes and a fedora, and a heavy baby-faced man with just wisps of hair on his shiny head wearing a T-shirt and running shorts. Everyone nods.

The black man in the hat says, "We'll say the Serenity Prayer in a couple minutes. We like to leave a space. In case anyone else wants to talk."

"Sometimes nobody does, though," Beth says.

"But other times they do," Vernon says.

There are sniffs. Chairs creak. Lynn's two dissimilar hands lie still in her lap, and she keeps her eyes on them.

Someone coughs.

Then the five of them say the Serenity Prayer without her.

In the dim garage Vivian is preparing bowls of food. It is two o'clock, and Lynn has not returned. So Vivian is thinking about the dogs and doing her best to remember how the older woman said it was done. She has forgotten the idea of doing it in the open, where it is brighter and already dirty, and she has the bowls lined up on the concrete floor, two rows of twelve, and she stands there in her flowered sundress and borrowed rubber boots and barn coat, can opener in hand.

Her babies are asleep again, and have been for hours. They woke briefly after the hunter's visit, but Vivian could tell from the way they fussed on the porch that they were spent from the long night awake and crying in her car. So she stretched them a bit, heaping their bunchy bodies one on each shoulder and walking an invisible castle wall around Lynn's keep—the dog yard and the shed and the barn in the distance that held a story the older woman didn't want to tell—and then she prepared their bottles and fed them in the living room, Sebastian and Emmaline sucking in the same sleepy way, their tiny eyelids closed, while Vivian considered the old computer in the corner that sits covered in plastic on a little table next to the potbellied stove. The babies fell asleep eating, and she laid them to sleep in their seats and afterward played a game of solitaire—a real one with Lynn's real cards instead of the game on Marco's phone—still considering.

Now she sets the can opener on the top of the can and draws the little pink cell phone from her pocket. The counter along the window where Lynn had prepared the vials of flea treatment has a row of high shallow windows above. It is the only natural light in the garage. Vivian draws a tiny scroll of paper from the pocket of her own sweatshirt and unfurls it on the scratched brown formica—a little two-inch scrap of torn yellow paper. She has to use two hands to roll it back against itself and make it lie flat. It is a phone number, written in handwriting that is round, almost puffy. She dials it and puts the sparkly little phone to her ear. One ring. Two. A woman's voice answers: "Carla Bonham."

Vivian doesn't speak. The windows above her head are all clouds and sky, and they make a pool of gold at the crown of her pale yellow hair.

"Hello?" the voice says.

Vivian hangs up.

She sets the phone on the counter in the sun and looks back at the cans of food. She walks back to the first can and picks up the opener and fits it on the rim. Click. A little juice spurts up through the first cut as she begins to turn. Her phone starts ringing on the counter, skittering a little with the vibration it makes, but Vivian does not look at it. She keeps twisting, the can opener making a cranking sound, shifting her feet and turning to rotate with it, the muscles in her hand working hard. When she has made it all the way around, she pulls back the ragged metal circle, revealing the pink-gray top of the loaf of meat.

The phone rings eight times before it stops. By then she has moved on to the third can, and she does not stop, not even after the phone makes a little beep to let her know she has new voice mail. She finishes opening the cans, and then she lifts one, tipping it, waiting for the food to slip out, shaking it a little and patting the side of the can when it does not. She sets the can down and looks around the room. There is a big stainless-steel scoop next to the kibble and Vivian does her best to use this, carving at the slick top of the meat and dumping the bits she carves free into the empty bowl. She looks down the row, planning, looking in the can to see whether she has served the right fraction, and then she moves on. Her way is messier than she'd like. She drips a little juice on her dress and leaves little bits of the meat on the floor of the garage, and she eyes each bit she drops with a furrowed brow. But she keeps moving along, setting a finished can aside until all of the bowls are full.

Then she sets about cleaning, first setting a can top next to each scrap in dustpan fashion and pulling the meat bits onto it with bunched fingertips, next trying a sponge that comes back from each dab on the dirty floor the color of coffee, and finally disappearing and returning minutes later with a bucket and mop and swabbing every inch of Lynn's garage, changing the rinse water six times, pouring it into the sink, a red-brown like bean liquor, until finally the whole floor is just a wet, dark gray.

She leans against the counter, wiping the sleeve of Lynn's coat across her forehead where her hair is damp, and surveys her work—all the bowls full at her back and the empty cans lined up against the wall and the floor so clean. Then she takes the phone off the windowsill to listen to the new message.

"Vivian? This is Carla Bonham. I'm so glad you tried calling me! I hope you'll try again and let me talk to you. I promise I can make it easy to tell me about it. I wouldn't rush you. And I'd give you a choice of answering or not with every question. Some girls like for me to write them down first so they can see the questions alone and think about them before they even meet me, and if you like I can do that for you too. I know you don't want to talk about it, and that you're scared, but it will be so much better than doing it under subpoena. Do you know what that is? You'd have to come by law and talk to me for the first time in front of him and everybody else. Wouldn't that be worse? But if you call me on the phone we can chat that way, just you and me, or maybe meet somewhere for a soda and talk about something else first so you can get a good look at me. Or start alone in a room in my office. Whatever feels safe and easy to you, so please, please try me again."

Vivian slips the phone back in the pocket of Lynn's barn coat and walks across the dark freshly washed floor and presses the big white button on the side of the garage. A crank above her rattles loudly, and the big double garage doors open, flooding the room by degrees with a bright white afternoon light. She can see all of Lynn's outbuildings laid out around the hard-baked turnaround. The shed, the dog yard, and the barn and the big empty cistern in the distance. And the dog yard has exploded with barking. They are all gathered up near the fence as she sets the bowls under the chain-link flap, bringing them two by two, lining them up with a bit of space between as the dogs bark—hound dogs baying low and the smaller ones sharp and high-pitched, some of them flipping circles as they watch her. When she gets the last pair placed she closes the outer hatch and hoists the rope, moving as quickly as she can to raise the panel and give them access to the bowls. Some of them crowd the first section she opens, but a few are smart enough to wait by the last one. There are squabbles, but soon enough all of them are eating, some of them gobbling, some taking dainty little bites, one setting pieces on the dry ground before picking them up again to eat them.

Vivian smiles. She sighs and rolls her neck to stretch it in the sun. Then she trudges back to the house in Lynn's boots and takes the last bowl from the garage and in the kitchen mixes puppy food in the blender like Lynn said to, reading the side of the milk-replacer can like she once had to for her own babies, and sets it on the clear plastic sheet in the dark living room. The mama dog heaves herself up and heads for it in the dim, the teats swaying below her, so many of them, and her puppies trotting and falling alongside her.

Her own babies are still asleep.

And her chores for Lynn are done.

She looks again at the computer in the corner. It has a layer of shaped plastic over it like some old people's couches, and when she pulls the plastic up and away, the screen flickers and she finds it has a browser window open to a page that says "Three Paws Dog Rescue," with pictures below of dogs she recognizes from the morning. Vivian's mother used to say that integrity means doing the right thing even when no one is there to see it, and right away Vivian closes that window because it is not hers, even though she guesses that it is just what Lynn puts up for all the world to see. It is the kind of thing kids at school made fun of her for. She couldn't help it, though. And anyway it was easier that last year at home not to have friends to keep secrets from, and now not to have them to miss.

She opens a fresh search window, Google with an empty box and a cursor blinking, and she watches it a second, her heart speeding up, and when she feels that she pauses a second to think about what she is doing. To make sure it is okay. It has been a long time that she has wanted to do this and not done it, but Marco didn't have a computer, and the phone he got her only had voice mail and a few games. That's the only reason she hasn't. Not because she felt it was wrong. She clicks on Images so what she'll get is pictures, and then in a rush she types "Carla Bonham Las Vegas," and the screen fills with a few different people but most of them a square-faced older woman with not very much makeup and soft brown hair smiling just a little bit. Closed lipped but nice-looking. Vivian scans through other pictures of people doing things—camping and bowling and a few in swimsuits—but those must be a different Carla. All she gets of Carla Bonham is her face.

Behind her the puppies lap and their nails click on the plastic. When she is finished looking, Vivian is careful to open Lynn's dog rescue window again, but also not to look at it, and to cover the computer the way she left it to keep off dust, and then she goes to the dark doorway and peers around the corner to see her babies, awake again now from the noise of dogs eating but quiet in their carriers, each of them playing with the plastic measuring spoons on their bellies where she knew to leave them.

Vivian picks their carriers up, lifts them past the mama dog and over the baby fencing. She takes them out into the sunlight and sets them on the porch and sits down on the steps beside them. They squint in the bright, and Vivian looks from the eating dogs to her quiet babies and says, "This is a pretty good place I found for us, isn't it?"

Sebastian's eyes widen at her, and he chomps down on the white plastic tablespoon, drooling. Emmaline raises her fistful of spoons and rattles it, kicking her legs.

Vivian laughs. "I think so too. I think that exactly. Just look at it." She sweeps a hand out over what she surveys—over the barn in the distance and the bustling dog yard and the garage full of food, and also meaning even the empty land beyond it all, all of Lynn's wide-open neighborless space, and Vivian takes it in, her gaze tripping over the state highway finally, where she sees a red car approaching and turning in down Lynn's drive.

She stands.

She snatches up both carriers and hurries into the house, into the dim of the living room past the mama dog and into the dark corner of the old bedroom and stashes her babies there on the floor. She hustles to the hall closet and reaches into the back row of the liquor carton and slips Lynn's gun into the pocket of the barn coat.

Then she steps back out onto the porch.

The red car is having trouble. It is a low-riding TransAm, made before Vivian was even born, the black wheel hubs exposed and the paint stripped down to its lusterless base coat, and its underbelly drags against the high spots in the drive, scraping rocks here and there. As it gets close Vivian can hear muffled cursing through the open driver's window, but when he gets out in his shiny track suit, he hitches the waist of his pants and grins.

Vivian crosses her arms.

He says, "What? You think I gave you that little pink phone only so I can call you up and tell you how pretty you are or see if you need more diapers?"

He's still smiling. He takes a few steps closer. "It good for that, sure, but I also want to make sure I don't lose track of the best thing ever happen to me. Didn't I say I would protect you?"

"Marco—" she says.

Behind her, from their place deep inside the house, she can hear the babies begin to cry.

She puts a hand out to stay his progress.

"Whoa now, girl, think a minute." He takes another couple steps toward the porch and stretches out both arms, palms turned up, but not smiling anymore. He is close enough now that Vivian can see the burn scars hiding inside his upturned collar. He says, "When you gone last night when I get back with my associates, standing like a fool listening to them say, 'Where she go, man? Where's this Pebbles? Where's this candy you been telling us about?' First I think, I'm going to have to teach her a lesson, and then I think, Wait a minute, no way could she have left on her own. Someone came"—he looks around him—"dogfighter or chicken rancher maybe, you tell me, but some cock knocker come and he try to take her away from me. Someone *make* her go. Now—you just tell Marco that's the way it went down, baby, and I won't hold it against you."

He steps onto the first porch step, and Vivian reaches into her pocket and pulls out Lynn's gun. She holds it out, trembling, and puts her other hand up to steady it.

Marco raises his eyebrows. "What's this?"

When she does not answer, or even move, he laughs. He doubles over, making a show of it, and Vivian watches, her jaw set and her arms shaking wildly.

Finally he rights himself and says, "Why don't you just toss that shit down to me before you hurt yourself. From up there with those jello arms you just as like to hit a dog as any part of me."

Vivian says, "I'm nervous, you got that right, but I've been practicing all morning. You look at that post over there with all the bullet holes in it and see if I haven't."

He glances over his shoulder and then back at her. The cries from inside the house are getting louder, and her arms are still shaking wildly.

"Come on, baby. If you such a good shot you must be shaking 'cause you don't want to shoot me. Put that down and let's go take care of those babies together. I'm thinking maybe we buy them a bed. Some toys to play with, maybe."

Her arms won't quit. They shake so much the gun appears to be vibrating. She begins to cry. Just water from her eyes, though. Her jaw is steady, her face blank, and her body does not respond to the swells of panic in her babies' cries. Her eyes do not even flick to the driveway at the sound of gravel crunching under the tires in the distance. Marco registers this, and because he understands that she will not, he turns to look.

Coming down the driveway is a yellow pickup truck. It stops in the center of the turnaround, and out hops Lynn holding her cell phone ahead of her in her good hand with the knuckling of rings. She is looking not at Marco's astonished face but at the phone screen as she presses a button.

"That's one for the yearbook," she says. Then she slips it in her pocket and pulls out a pistol and aims it right at his face.

"So. Romeo. Looks to me like my new friend Vivian wants you to leave."

Marco raises his hands for the first time and turns to the side between their two guns. "All right, ladies. I don't want no trouble."

Lynn says, "That's what I thought. Let me tell you about some, though. Whatever she may have told you, that girl is fifteen years old and when she showed up this morning she had a garbage bag full of dirty laundry. I saved out every pair of panties in it just like Monica Lewinsky's mommy, and I just drove them to my safe-deposit box in Boulder City. Whatever you got going, I'm sure it won't help to be wanted for statutory rape, so even though you know her new address, you are never coming back."

He moves to step down the stairs as if she is ready to let him leave, but she cocks the gun with her thumb.

He stops.

"And I'll tell you what else," she says. "I called some of my girlfriends in Vegas and told them the whole story and then put my spare safe-deposit key in a little padded mailer and sent it to them for safekeeping. Anything happens to either one of us and you are in for a world of shit because I'm Facebooking your mug shot just as soon as you back your junk out onto the highway."

"No need, no need for any of that, Cagney, I ain't coming back," he says, his hands calming the air, and Lynn tracks him with the barrel of her gun as he gets into his car and starts his engine, and then he looks out the window at her and grins. "That mall parking lot like a stocked pond. I won't come back for this fish."

She lets him go.

On the porch Vivian lowers her gun, watching him back away, but she sees that out in the center circle of her property, Lynn does not. Not until he's out on the highway and gone. Then she uncocks her pistol and climbs into her truck to put it back in the lockbox in her glove compartment.

When Lynn backs out of the cab of her truck, she sees that Vivian is gone from the porch and that the sound of crying has stopped. Instead she hears singing. Dipping and rising, a seesaw melody she remembers. She goes inside and finds Vivian standing in the dim of the mama dog's room holding a baby in each arm, the clear plastic dimpled under her weight, the puppies behind her as she pivots back and forth, back and forth, singing "Bicycle Built for Two" in a voice that is still shaky.

"Are they hungry?" Lynn says.

Vivian nods, still singing and swaying.

"I'll fix bottles for them," Lynn says.

She can still hear the girl's voice in the next room as she turns on the heat under the empty saucepan on the stove and fills it from the cold kettle. "Daisy, Daisy . . . " She washes her hands at the sink, flipping the sliver of yellow soap over and over in her right palm and then cleaning the loops of metal too. The formula container is where she left it earlier that morning, between the blender and her puzzle books. The baby bottles and nipples lie on a fresh towel on the counter where the girl must have laid them after she cleaned them. Lynn measures the scoops of yellow-white powder into the bottles and adds water to the line as Vivian told her to. "I'm half crazy. . . ." The girl sings, and the pot of water at Lynn's back makes a soft hissing noise that sounds like sighing.

When the water in the stove pot begins to boil, Lynn checks the bottles, pouring a little from each nipple onto her wrist, and it feels just right. She leaves the bright kitchen, passing through the dark front hall and into the cavelike living room with its drawn shades. Vivian is taking a pillow and setting it at the edge of the first couch cushion and settling there, and when Lynn holds out the bottles in the dim she accepts them, craning her wrists to fit them neatly into the babies' mouths.

She stops singing now, and Lynn stands there a moment above her, listening more than watching in the dark. Little smacking sounds of the babies' lips; a ticking of pressure in one of the bottles; the shift of the mama dog on the plastic sheet. As her eyes begin to adjust she can see better the outline of the girl with her babies, and her own boots next to the girl's and the baby fencing. Finally she sees her pistol lying there on the end table next to an unfinished game of solitaire, the rows of red and black building up, the four suits interlacing. She picks up the gun and takes it back to the front hall where the coat closet door is still ajar, the spare boots lie downed like bowling pins, the carton of Jack Daniel's boxes pulled out to the threshold, one lying open-flapped in the back row. Lynn sets the safety and then slides it down in.

She fixes a pot of coffee and takes a blue enamel mug from a hook and sets it on the counter. She pours it most of the way full, and takes a spoon from the drawer and stirs it, tinkling the sides of the cup with a shaking hand and staring at an empty whiskey bottle on a high shelf next to her puzzle books. She reaches up and past it, and pulls out from behind it a stick of yellow paper—a sheet of legal pad folded and folded and folded until it is so thin it could be slipped in a bottle. She stares at it a moment and thumbs a furled edge, but she doesn't open it. She sets it back in the corner and the bottle in front of it, just as it was. Then she opens a cupboard and takes out a sleeve of rice cakes and a jar of natural peanut butter and she fixes herself a snack, spreading a thin layer with the knife. She takes a bite, crunching and licking her lips clean of the sticky butter as she looks down into her dark coffee.

She is sitting on the top porch step with the mostly uneaten rice cake and her cup of coffee when Vivian finds her. The girl does not sit down right away herself, but stands just behind and to the side, one hand on the post that supports the low roof above them, and before she can speak, Lynn stands and drains her coffee cup in one long draught. "It's time we tended to Sweetie Pie."

"Sweetie Pie?"

Lynn sets the mug on the porch rail and clomps down the steps to the rear of her pickup. When Vivian meets her there, she is looking in through the dirty brown window of the camper shell. She says, "If you open it slowly, I can reach in through the crack for the leash and catch her before she jumps out."

She doesn't wait for Vivian to answer. She pops the release on the tailgate, and then moves her hands down to the opening, leaving Vivian to catch it as it falls, which Vivian does. There is no sound from inside, and when it is open, there unmoving lies a young dog with long silky red hair and a basket muzzle.

"There we go," Lynn says, that sweet soft voice returning. She draws the leash forward as the door opens, and the dog jumps down onto the dry rutted earth.

Vivian says, "Why does she have a muzzle on?"

Lynn keeps her eyes on the dog. In her normal voice she says, "They say she bit an attendant at the shelter. That doesn't necessarily mean anything, though. Locked up in a strange place and blind to boot? Some dogs will do fine once they're in a familiar environment and see a pattern of kind treatment. We'll put her in a separate pen right next to the other dogs and see how she does—whether she growls or draws back or seeks them out. She'll be able to get used to the smell of them, and have a little nose-to-nose contact with them along the line. It will help us decide whether she can mix with them."

The dog holds perfectly still between them, the leash slack and her long hair shining. Lynn says, "Why don't you go ahead and clear the path of things she might trip on. That hose near the water troughs, for one."

Vivian holds two hands up like a shed roof over her eyes and sees it—

a green coil in the path to a small fenced area she had not noticed before on the far side of the pen. She walks ahead in Lynn's big boots and squats to drag it across the concrete, and moves a plastic garbage bin as well, and the shovel Lynn uses for cleaning up after the dogs. Then she waits at the fence Lynn showed her—a high eight-by-four rectangle of chain-link that shares one of its walls with the far boundary of the dog yard.

Other dogs approach the water line as Lynn and the new dog pass, Lynn cooing, "Good girl, that's a good girl, you're such a big beautiful girl," all in her high sweet gentle voice. Some of them bark, and the blind dog lowers her head at the noise. She stumbles only once, on the lip of the concrete as she approaches. Vivian stands aside to let her get to the door, and once she is in, Lynn takes a handful of moist-looking treats from her pocket and lays them on the dry earth. "There we go, Sweetie Pie. Those are for you. Isn't this a good place? Can't you tell how much I care about you? Can you tell how much I want to help you? I'm going to take such good care of you." Then in one swift motion, Lynn unfastens the buckle behind her ears, steps out of the pen, and the basket muzzle slips forward a bit and the dog paws at it, pushing it aside and off so she can eat the treats.

Lynn watches the dog, and Vivian watches Lynn.

Sweetie Pie is sniffing along the ground now near the chain-link, at the nose of a Border collie. Their noses touch and press against each other and then separate, sniffing. The Border collie barks, and then they repeat it. Lynn goes on staring, although she can see now that Vivian is looking at her, watching her watch.

"I'm sorry he came here," the girl says.

Lynn waves a hand to bat the thought away, keeping her eyes on the dogs.

Vivian says, "I didn't ever think that would happen. I didn't know he could find me. He did it from my cell phone, he said."

Sweetie Pie is nosing along the fence line inch by inch now, turning the corner and continuing to sniff, getting her sightless bearings.

Vivian says, "How did you know he was my boyfriend?"

"I didn't. But if I was wrong, then I was just an old crazy lady, which I'm perfectly willing to be." She turns toward the house and starts walking. "You hungry?"

Vivian follows her. "Plus I probably look like just the type who would make a mistake like him," she says morosely.

"Oh, well, 'mistake.' Who doesn't make those? Do you like rice cakes?"

"I'm older than you said I was, too—seventeen. Old enough to know better."

"Well, there's no age cutoff for stumbling." She starts up the porch steps and grabs her empty mug. "How about peanut butter?"

"And now he knows where you live."

"Or chips and bean dip?"

"Even if I leave right now, that stays behind."

"I have cereal too," Lynn says, opening the screen door. "All kinds of cold cereal, but you have to tolerate soy milk. You just tell me what sounds good."

In the kitchen Vivian flops down in a chair, and Lynn sets her coffee mug in the sink and opens all the cupboards. "Bean burritos?"

She doesn't look at Vivian, who is holding her head in her hands at the table. She plows on, "Or I could do another shake if you liked it at all."

Vivian says, "I've been enough trouble already."

Lynn ignores her, pulling out a box of granola and another of corn flakes. She takes the sleeve of rice cakes and the jar of peanut butter from where she left it on the counter and sets it in front of the girl. She opens the refrigerator and sets out a Tupperware of what looks to be rice. Then a little bowl of berries. A half-gallon carton of soy milk. A jar of marmalade and a loaf of grainy bread. A bowl of lettuce and a little green plastic basket of cherry tomatoes. A can of olives from the cupboard. A can of black beans. A can of vegetable soup.

She is still heaping pantry items on the table around the girl's bowed head when Vivian's cell phone rings. Lynn does not stop moving at the sound of it. She turns to the coffeemaker, her hands shaking, and refills the mug she had set in the sink. Then she stares down into it. She takes a spoon from the drawer and begins stirring. On the fifth ring she glances over her shoulder, and she sees that Vivian is crying.

Lynn says, "No way should you answer that phone. And don't go calling him back later either. What I did will stick but not if you chat with him, not even one time to say stop calling. Like a dog he will just learn that the price of a table scrap is thirty-five unanswered phone calls. Next thing you know he'll be working to figure a way to get you to meet him somewhere."

Vivian's head is bowed over the circle of her arms, tears spotting the sleeves of Lynn's big coat, the food she does not want to eat arrayed all around her. She has not taken the cell phone from her pocket and when it stops ringing, she does not look up.

In all this time Lynn has not stopped stirring her coffee, and the tinkling sound of it seems ridiculous suddenly, and she makes herself stop. She stares at the girl.

There is a faint beep in the pocket of her borrowed coat.

Lynn says, "And you should erase those messages without even listening to them. It doesn't matter what he said. They'll just confuse you."

Vivian holds very still over her tears, but Lynn can see they are still falling.

Then the phone starts ringing again, and the girl lets out a little moan of despair.

Lynn says, "He'll stop. I promise you he will, but not if you don't follow that advice."

Vivian says, "It's not Marco."

Her voice is so small that Lynn can't be sure she heard her correctly. "What now?"

Vivian buries her head in her arms. "It's not him, none of them have been. It's somebody else."

"You can use the same method with any of them."

"It's not a man. And it will be worse if she stops calling."

Vivian buries her head and starts sobbing now, and Lynn takes a step forward and sits down across from her at the table. She pushes the food aside and lays her good hand on Vivian's shoulder.

"There now," she says. The girl's shoulders are shaking. Lynn looks at the shining top of her head, the hair shifting. "I'm a pretty old lady, and I've had plenty of time to make mistakes of my own to learn from." She briefly closes her eyes. She says, "What you asked about before— I was just a little older than you when I lost this hand." She gives Vivian a pat. "I lost it trying to help a boy who was only pretending to love me." Vivian stops sobbing. She holds very still but does not look up. Lynn pats her again. "Why don't you tell me the whole story, and I'll see if I can help you figure out how to set it right."

It is dusk when Lynn walks up the narrow stairs with fresh sheets. She begins in the room she sleeps in herself, stripping the little twin bed along the wall and laying it with a clean white one and a new yellow blanket to replace the dark old corduroy spread that made it look like a couch. Although she had never done it for herself, she takes the sewing machine off the desk and sets it in the closet. She removes the dusty shoebox of spools. She runs her old pillowcase across the surface of the desk, felting it with gray dust, and lays a little vase of flowers on top, figuring the girl might put things there, like the girls before her did downstairs. Last she takes her puzzle books from the edge, and the empty juice glass and bottle from the drawer underneath, and finally the manila envelope, and she places them gently into the shoebox with the spools.

She goes to the bathroom next and takes her toothbrush from the cabinet, and a pale blue plastic hairbrush, and loads them in with the bottle and the spools. She takes a long strand of her gray hair from the soap dish. The rest of the bathroom looks clean enough, but she knows it must not be. So she makes it clean. She wipes the counter down and lifts the yellow bar of soap and rinses the dish out in the sink. From the shelf above she takes a fresh towel and puts it on the bar next to the claw-footed tub.

Out in the narrow hall with her shoebox, she faces the white-painted door. It makes a sticking sound when she opens it, the paint of the frame sealed tight to the paint of the door. There is a desk long ago cleared, and on the wall is a bulletin board trimmed in white eyelet ribbon, bare but for a few pushpins stuck into the cork. The closet door stands open, and there are hangers there, but no clothes.

The room itself is mostly pink: a twin bed with a rosebud bedspread, pink-dotted walls. An old pink-painted doll crib is stuffed with animals and pink-dressed dolls. The bed is a daybed with white-painted iron rails on three sides, and Lynn stands for a moment looking down at its lace-trimmed pillows. There is dust on the spread. Dust on the floor. Dust on the dresser.

She steps to the window and slides the sash open, letting in the sound of barking dogs. The round rag rug on the floor when she hangs it out and beats it on the side of the house releases a cloud of dust so thick it looks almost celebratory, like confetti, and she does the same with the bedspread, and then rests them over the sill while she sweeps the floor, filling a dustpan with dust and emptying it out the open window. Then she puts everything back into place, taking time to make it neat and square.

Downstairs Lynn sets the shoebox on the kitchen table. Then she goes to get the girl. The two nursers lie empty on the side table by the couch under the one lit lamp, and Lynn finds her standing in the far corner, in the dark of the bedroom, patting the girl on the shoulder to burp her while she rocks the boy in the car seat on the floor with her foot. Lynn just watches for a moment, the baby girl watching her with shining eyes over Vivian's shoulder, and when she finally bends to lay her too into the other car seat, Lynn steps forward to help.

"Upstairs," she whispers. "I have a better place."

She picks up one of the car seats herself, the girl's, and Vivian picks up the boy's and follows. The stairs creak as they rise. She points to the sewing room as she passes and says, "You'll sleep in there, so you can be close enough to hear them," and then she takes a step farther, to the end of the hall, and into the room with the white-painted door.

When Vivian steps in behind her she sees that Lynn has nestled the girl's car seat among the pillows on the daybed. And she is saying, "When they're ready for it, this bed has a side rail that can flip up and latch to make it more like a crib." But Vivian is not really looking there yet. She is taking in the room.

"You had a girl of your own."

"Yes," Lynn says.

The baby girl is making a winding-up noise. Vivian sets the boy's seat on the floor and goes to lift her.

"I'll leave you to tend to them your own way," Lynn says. "You let me know if you need anything, though. I'll be downstairs."

"Where is your room?"

"Next to the mama dog's, where you had them before."

"That's your bedroom?"

"It was a long time ago."

Lynn doesn't wait for her to object. She goes down the stairs. She goes into the kitchen and picks up the shoebox. Then she goes to the living room and steps over the rail, crinkling over the plastic, and over the baby gate again into the dark beyond, where she reaches for a wall switch and turns on a lamp on either side of the big queen bed with a wooden footboard carved with leaves and grapes. She takes the puzzle books from her box and lays them on the nightstand. Then she sets the manila envelope in her lap.

It is furred along its edges, like felt, with age, but it is clear that it has not been opened. The flap is held closed with a metal clasp, and also sealed, and straddling the seam of the seal is her own signature from long ago. She pinches open the metal clasp. Then she works her thumb under the flap and tears it open slowly, inching, as if the tearing sound itself is painful, and then she sets her hand on the bedspread to gather herself.

She firms her lips.

Above her she can hear the creak of floorboards as Vivian walks about, settling herself in the spare room.

Finally she grasps the envelope again and stands it on its end in her lap and looks down at the edge of the papers inside. Some of them are thick, like photographs, some have the narrow cream edges of stationery paper, and some the pulpy gray of newsprint.

Her fingers tremble as she withdraws the stack and sets it in her lap. On top is an obituary page from the *Southern Nevada Gazette* dated October 29, 1972.

Raymond L. Doran, 43, and Marion F. Doran, 39, passed away in an automobile accident near their dairy farm north of Searchlight.

Ray was born on February 28, 1929, in Albuquerque to Jim and Sara Doran, and was the devoted older brother of Macy and Ed. He graduated from Citrus Hill High School and Texas A&M University and was a member of the Lincoln County volunteer fire department. He loved farm work, playing the guitar, telling a joke, and making pancakes for his wife and daughter.

Marion was born on April 19, 1933, in El Paso to Owen and Clara Eastman, and was the loving younger sister of Tim, Peter, and Ginny. She graduated from Walt Whitman High School and Texas A&M and was a volunteer at the Lincoln County animal shelter. She loved baking, dogs, and spending time with friends and family.

The couple was happily married 20 years, and touched the lives of many people with their kindness. They are survived by their parents, their siblings, and their 17-year-old daughter, Lynn.

Services are being coordinated by Marion's sister Ginny Falkes of Easton, and will be held graveside on Saturday at 11 am at the Big Rock Cemetery with Reverend Elland officiating.

She smooths a fold at the bottom edge of the clipping with her thumb. And another along the side.

The floorboards creak again above her.

A puppy whimpers in its sleep in the next room.

She decides it's enough for now—a start. She fits the papers back in the envelope and closes it again with just the clasp and sets it inside the box. Then she takes a marker from the drawer below and along the box of spools with her empty bottle and juice glass she writes "Lynn" and opens the closet door, and sets it on the top shelf with the others.

Now she sits down on the bed. The posters are of three boys standing shoulder to shoulder and a girl alone with a guitar. She looks at them a moment. Then she stands and one by one she takes each tack out of the wall to remove them. They make a crashing sound as they fall, like cartoon thunder, all folding up on the floor, and the puppies stir on the plastic sheet, scrabbling to see, and Lynn knows as they do not that it is like going back in time, each layer recalling a different set of practice dreams: the Jonas Brothers and Taylor Swift, Madonna and Matt Dillon, Marilyn Monroe and James Dean.

When they have all fallen away, underneath there are just a few photos tacked there. One of herself in a wedding dress next to a man with shining eyes and dark hair combed slick with a product of some kind. Another of her in a hospital bed, laughing and surrounded by roses. A third of a little girl crouching over red earth and drawing in it with a stick. The breath Lynn draws in and pushes back out is firm, like a decision. She takes off her necklace. She takes off her sweater and the plastic and metal hand. She removes her pants and slips under the covers with her puzzle book and pen and looks around the room she used to sleep in.

8

Injuries

Waiting for her turn in the Emergency Room, Jessica feels an ironic sense of safety. Although somewhere above her, in an air-conditioned chamber at the heart of this enormous hospital, her father lies waiting for her, this cannot be where he was expecting her to arrive. Here she is still safe. Velasquez has taken a seat by the door, leaving her to check in alone, which she does under her married name, keeping her sunglasses on and looking distractedly down at her BlackBerry. The bored girl at the desk doesn't even look up from her keyboard before releasing her to sit in one of the orange plastic chairs lined up along the wall. The room is almost empty—just a sunburned man in golf clothes pressing an icepack to his head and a heavy black woman patting an elderly white woman's hand, each of whom disappears quickly when a young ponytailed nurse in scrubs cracks open a swinging door with her clipboard and calls them inside. Then it is Jessica's turn, and the nurse does not look at Jessica, or examine her hand, or ask Velasquez if he is kin, just expects them to trail her down the hall past the gurneys and wheeled IV stands and people rushing around heads down in their scrubs and into a room where she makes straight for a laptop on the counter and taps away as she asks her bland questions (date of birth, allergies, insurance) and then washes Jessica's hand briskly over a sink, never even looking at her face, before disappearing into the hall. This is too easy, Jessica thinks. And also, wistfully, *This is passing too fast.* She sits down on the crinkly paper-covered table, gazing through her sunglasses at her puffy, bluish hand with a sinking feeling, until the doctor appears.

Jessica hears her before she sees her, clicking loudly down the hall on what turns out to be a pair of kitten-heeled leopard-print pumps: a big-boned Asian woman with a thick ponytail and diamond studs in her ears. The hem of a herringbone skirt peeks out from under her white lab coat.

"Ouch!" she says. She steps right up to Jessica, standing almost between her knees, and takes her hand by the fingertips. "So much for man's best friend. Wiggle for me." Jessica wiggles. "Good. Can you make a fist? Nice. And flex out like this? Okay, good." She clicks across the room to the counter where Velasquez is standing. She opens a jar on the counter and takes out a long wood-shafted Q-tip. She leans back against the counter, crosses her ankles, and snaps the Q-tip in half neatly. She points a thumb at Velasquez. "Husband?"

"Friend," Jessica says.

The doctor narrows her eyes at Jessica in her sunglasses, and then at Velasquez. "If you say so. Okay, pop quiz, bosom buddies. There were zero cases of human rabies in Nevada last year, and only one in the whole country, and that one wasn't transmitted by a dog, it was a bat, which is typical. Mostly these days it's bats. And what's the number-one risk factor for death from a bat bite? You first." She looks squarely at Jessica.

"I don't know."

"Guess."

"I don't have any idea."

"Guess anyway."

"Um . . ."

The doctor rolls her eyes and turns to Velasquez. "Your turn, big boy."

"Not seeking treatment," he says.

The doctor raises her hand toward him for a high five, still looking at Jessica, still leaning against the counter with her thick ankles crossed and her polished shoes gleaming. Velasquez waits to see if she will give up, and when she does not he meets her palm without enthusiasm, and she lowers her hand.

"Top shelf of the carny booth! Get this boy a jumbo monkey! Yes—the damn things move so fast, and the bites are tiny and painless, so mostly people don't even know they've been bitten. Bottom line is, if you've spent any time with a bat, you need help. Code red. Inside there's a chance you're already dying. Stand up and take off your hat and sunglasses for me."

For a moment Jessica does not realize this is not part of her lesson on bat bites. But when the doctor stares at her, waiting, she slips off the table and removes her hat with her left hand. With her injured one she pulls off her sunglasses, keeping her head bowed and staring down at the dark lenses as if they are somehow important.

It makes the doctor look at them too. "Chanel—nice! Check out my shoes."

She holds one shiny leopard-print toe out and turns her thick ankle this way and that, and Jessica nods appreciatively. She lowers her foot and meets Jessica in the center of the room to take her by the wrist. "With dogs, not so much. If they hurt you, they make it extremely clear. They warn you with growling, give you a good hard bite, no secret poisons. Here, let me hold those for you a minute so I can test that hand." She takes the glasses and slips them in the patch pocket of her lab coat. "Now: do me a favor and turn your palm up but don't look at it, look only at my eyes."

Jessica raises her head.

"Rice and beans! You're Jessica Lessing!"

Jessica gives her a tight smile. The doctor's face is so close to hers she can smell the coffee on her breath.

"Your dad's on two. Everyone's switched from talking about last night's *Dancing with the Stars* to talking about whether you'll come visit him. Have you seen him yet?"

Jessica looks down at her hand, and the doctor's fingers encircling her wrist. "No."

"He's a real piece of work. I've got one just like him, so I feel for you. Total bilker. First-class flimflammer. Grade A deceiver. Coldhearted snake." She holds her left fist out above Jessica's wounded hand. "Blow it up for epically shitty childhoods."

After a startled second Jessica holds her left fist up to meet it, and the doctor pops open her fist and shoots her fingers waggling in victory toward the fluorescent ceiling, and then lowers them to rest on her hip. In her other hand she still has Jessica by the wrist.

"So is Arjawal your married name?"

"Yes."

"Where's hubby from?"

"Orange County. But his parents are from Mumbai."

"Computer scientist? Lab scientist? Doctor?"

"Doctor. An ER doctor, actually."

"Ha! Well you can tell him you won the Podunk ER doctor lottery on this one. I graduated 4.0 from Johns Hopkins, and I vaccinated a hundred and seventy-five bat-bite victims for rabies on a Doctors Without Borders trip to Peru. I only picked Summerlin for the sun, spas, and the low-date-frequency bachelors—gamblers, golfers, comedy clubbers. I love a man who's only in town to love me once a month. Now: tell me whether each of these touches feels sharp or dull. But no peeking. Look only at me." Jessica looks up at her, and the urge to look away is almost irresistible. She quells it by making a study of her irises, which are so dark they are almost indistinguishable from her pupils. It is ironic how much she hates a closeup. But when she is acting she is someone else. The pain she might feel or cause in any exchange is not hers. There is nothing to regret. The first part she read for was in high school. She had just that week extracted herself from her father's apartment by moving into a spare bedroom she saw advertised on a handwritten flyer on the bulletin board in the cafeteria, and the only rent turned out to be child care her landlords summoned by knocking on her door at odd hours and handing her their toddler so they could go in the kitchen and fight. The audition manager asked her to read something from a book of monologues, Alison's lost-baby speech from *Look Back in Anger,* and when she cried onstage at the end, the boy reading Jimmy for her cried too, and so did the director in her folding chair below, but afterward instead of apologies and averted glances, there was only applause.

Staring into the doctor's eyes she feels unnerved and vulnerable in a way that she never does in front of a camera or onstage. The doctor presses the broken tip to the pad below her thumb.

"Sharp," Jessica tells her.

"Good girl." She flips the tip around and presses below her index finger.

"Dull."

The doctor moves along this way, testing her, looking frankly into Jessica's pale blue eyes, and then says, "Bingo." She taps the pedal on a step can with the toe of her shoe and drops the broken swab inside. "Your nerves are fine. Now—about Cujo. Where'd you find this cuddle bunny?"

Jessica tries to keep her face neutral. "About half a mile from here."

"Have you called Animal Control to report it?"

"No."

"We should do that." She pulls a cell phone from her pocket. "We're required to report bites by loose animals."

Jessica says, "Wait."

The doctor raises her eyebrows.

Jessica says, "She's not a stray."

"I thought you told the intake nurse you were worried about rabies."

"I just thought it was worth checking."

"Isn't she current on her shots?"

"I'm not sure."

"Did you ask the owner?"

"No."

"Let's call them, then." She holds out her iPhone, but Jessica hesitates. The doctor's face is smooth and unblinking. The diamonds wink in her ears. She is frank-faced and sharp-eyed, scanning Jessica like some kind of animal herself, alert for clues, and so quick that before Jessica can even compose a response, she says: "Holy crap, it's your dad's dog isn't it?"

"Yes."

"He's like your own personal Book of Exodus, this guy."

A puff of nervous laughter escapes Jessica. She clears her throat.

The doctor says, "No worries." She slips her phone back in her pocket. "I can figure it out without a shot record. Was the bite provoked or unprovoked?"

"I wasn't mistreating her, if that's what you mean."

"This isn't *Hard Copy*, Pretty Woman. 'Provoked' for a dog is anything that involves a biscuit. Were you feeding her?"

"Yes."

"Okay: provoked. And how's she now?"

"All right. Lying muzzled in a friend's car."

"What are friends for?" She glances at Velasquez with a tucked smile and then looks back at Jessica and winks. "So that's plenty. You should quarantine her for ten days. If she gets sick or acts strange before the days are up, we should test her to see if she's got rabies so we know whether to treat you." She takes a roll of gauze from a drawer and begins wrapping Jessica's hand, standing close. Jessica reads the ID badge dangling from a lanyard around her neck: Lisa Kim.

"Can't we test her now?"

"Sure, but we'd have to cut off her head and send it to a lab."

"Oh, God."

"That's what everybody says—'Poor Cujo! We mustn't harm Cujo!'" She finishes the bandage, almost a mitten now, and tapes it off. "But if she starts acting weird, don't go all Jain monk on me. At that point you definitely have to call and take her in for the ax. Can you do that?"

"Sure."

"Really?"

"Yes." She finds herself smiling.

"Because your symptoms would be next, and by the time they show up, it would be too late for you. There's no treatment after the onset of symptoms, it's just final makeup for you and everyone else that bitch bites, so there's no wait-and-see. Any questions?"

"No." Jessica shakes her head and smiles more fully. She feels light-headed around this woman suddenly, almost tipsy. "Thanks for helping me."

"No problem," she says. She takes the iPhone back out of her pocket. "Free with insurance copay and a photo for my tabloid blog."

Jessica feels herself tighten again, and Velasquez takes a step forward.

"Kidding!" she says. "Give me a cell phone number, and I'll go upstairs and do a little recon for you. Check around your dad's room and make sure there aren't any orderlies hanging around with their cell phone cameras."

Velasquez gives her a number, and she types it in.

"Got it." She looks at Jessica. "It was a pleasure meeting you. Keep up the Advil. And look up quarantine guidelines on the Health Department website. Don't mess around. The odds are super low, but starting an epidemic of rabies would be a lot of years of bad juju."

"And an *Us Weekly* cover besides," Jessica says, surprising herself, and Dr. Kim explodes with laughter.

"Damn, I'm a good doctor." Then she looks at Velasquez. "Okay. So you know Dad's room number already, I assume."

"Yes, ma'am."

"I'll call you in two," she says and she clicks out the door.

Only after she is gone does Jessica realize Dr. Kim still has her sunglasses. The urge to put them on is an instinct that doesn't die easily. She thinks next to put on her hat, but instantly she recognizes that threading her ponytail through its hole is something she can't manage with her bandaged hand. At last she moves to put her hands in her pockets, but she has the hat to hold and the bandage Dr. Kim gave her is much too large, and she is left to hold her arms at her sides like Dana and Velasquez, exposed but ready for whatever might come next.

Through the open door she hears water running. A tray clattering. Sneakers squeaking from one room to another. Velasquez's phone rings.

He presses a button and listens for a few seconds. "Thanks," he says. Then he presses a button again and slips it back in his pocket. He looks out the door and up and down the hallway and nods at her before going out so she knows she can follow. And it turns out the hat and sunglasses weren't needed after all. They move quickly down the empty hall, past an empty gurney and a rack of bedpans and boxes of surgical gloves and a row of IV stands and into an empty stairwell. She follows him up, watching his eyes pan up and down and around corners, everywhere but on her, and he opens a door on the second floor and checks in both directions and nods again, leading her down another empty hallway to a blond wood door with a brushed stainless-steel handle. The door is very smooth. The handle is the kind you push down on. This is what she will have to do to go in.

"This is it," he says. His brown shaved head shines in the fluorescent light. His face is friendly in a neutral way that strikes her as so kind and tactful she feels a lump in her throat. Akhil was wrong. Into his absence has stepped one surprising ally after another, like a path of stones.

She says, "Do you know if it's a shared room or private?"

"Private," he says.

Jessica pushes down on the door handle, releasing the latch with a click, and Velasquez nods. He will not try to follow her here. She pushes open the door just enough to slip through, and she disappears inside.

The room is small, suffused with light from a south-facing window, and so full of cords and tubes and monitors with blinking lights that it takes a moment for her eyes to adjust and narrow her focus to the center of the room and see that her father is sleeping. Overweight beneath the sheet, his jaw slack, his skin powdery pale, his orangey-brown dyed hair looking brittle against the pillowcase and revealing its silvered roots. Two little circles of buff-colored tape on his collarbone and two on his forehead, both with wires coming out and hooking him up to a machine. The open neckline of a peach-colored cotton dressing gown he must hate. The window behind him shows a broad swath of blue sky. She looks at him breathing shallowly, his big belly rising and falling beneath the sheet, and feels a strange sense of anticlimax. She had been bracing herself for his attack, armoring herself, talking herself up. Now she has to wait. She looks at her watch. She thinks about touching him and shaking him, and then she sees the chart at the end of his bed.

She takes it off its hook and examines it:

Name: Gabriel Fletcher
Date of Birth: April 20, 1950
Condition: Subdural hematoma, 14 days unresponsive

At first she imagines it is within his power to fake this too. She puts a hand on his powdery white arm with its pale gray hairs, and nothing inside him stirs. Not even a twitch behind his eyelids. She shakes him, gently at first, and then enough to make his big belly move. She reaches up finally and opens one wrinkled eyelid with her fingertip, and the ice blue iris stares up at the ceiling like the eye of a fish.

She jerks back her hand, and the lid slides shut slowly. You could say it sinks.

Jessica shakes her head. She wrinkles her forehead, and her lip trembles. She puts her mittened hand on her hip, scowling, watching his belly rise and fall. Then her eyes grow glassy. She looks back out the window, at the empty blue sky. She looks at him again. There are tiny spots on his skin, larger and more misshapen than freckles, from age. The skin on his jaw and beneath his nose shows a peppering of gray stubble, and the skin at his neck is so slack that it pools a bit to either side on the pillow, like the neck skin of certain lizards. She opens his eye again with her fingertips and looks at the cold blue iris. She notices that there is a thin limn of color at the border, almost green, like weathered copper. Tears stream down her cheeks. She looks at his mouth and sees that there is a rim of pearly pink inside, and that the lips themselves are so dry they are cracked, flaked with spittle at both corners. She reaches into her pocket and pulls out her chapstick. She uncaps it, her own lip trembling, and with her big bandaged hand reaches out and puts it on him, his mouth collapsing a bit, the lips crumpling and slipping off to the side as she pulls, but she doesn't withdraw. She does both lips, coating them thickly with the waxy balm, and then she recaps it.

There is a knock at the door then, and Jessica starts and slips the chapstick in her pocket, as if she has been caught at something illicit. The door opens, and Velasquez admits a man not much younger than her father. His hair is white and his tan hands, sticking out from the sleeves of his lab coat and gripping a clipboard, are wrinkled and corded like the root of a tree. "Excuse me," he says, and Velasquez lets the door close behind him. Jessica braces herself, although she is not sure for what kind of blow, or from what point of view she expects him to deliver it. As a doctor, a reprimand for applying chapstick? As a tabloid reader, brusque treatment for being so spoiled and cold? As an old man, a tone of disappointment for being less attentive than the daughter he'd want at his own deathbed? He is fit and wiry, like Akhil's father, so perhaps she is merely bracing herself for some of Akhil's father's oblivious frankness; he stumbles over people so frequently with his observations and advice that his wife and children have developed deep stores of eye-rolling good humor and skins the enviable thickness of bark. The doctor starts to raise a hand to shake Jessica's, but when he sees her enormous bandage, he lowers his hand and smiles. "I'm Dr. Stern," he says. "I've been treating your dad for the last week."

"I'm so sorry," Jessica blurts.

The man's brow knits sympathetically. "What for?"

So many things. But what she says is: "I was probably supposed to ask before coming in here."

Dr. Stern shrugs. "It's not that uncommon. It's not a moment in life when people think about asking permission. I'd probably do the same myself," he says. "Even without your complications."

After the pictures her father took of her children appeared in *People* magazine, there was an episode of *Hard Copy* where he pleaded on-screen for her to pick up the phone and call the studio so he could explain. After that even reviews of her films devoted at least a paragraph to the spectacle of her family life. Jessica feels a rush of gratitude toward this man. She thinks with relief of her sunglasses in Dr. Kim's pocket, not just an acceptable loss now but a lucky accident, as if she has narrowly missed stumbling into a mosque in a tank top. She wants to thank him for all the ways in which he has just been kind (empathy, candor, tact . . .), but she is afraid if she tries to name them she'll start to cry. She swallows. "Thanks," she manages finally.

Dr. Stern says, "Do you have any questions?"

Her throat clots again with tears at the magnitude of this opening. He puts on a pair of reading glasses, just to prepare to look at her father's chart, of course, but in the context of this moment it makes him look so like the magical wise old man from a fairy tale, her mind swims with inappropriate questions: *Why doesn't my dad love me? How long before I ruin my daughters? What am I doing wrong?* She looks out the window to collect herself, and after a few seconds something small enough to ask occurs to her.

"How did it happen?"

"We're not sure. A random person driving by his house called 911 from a cell phone. He was lying in his front yard. There was some trauma to his head. He may have tripped—I understand the yard was unfinished and full of holes."

The room has surprisingly little in it. A white vinyl stool on chrome wheels. That machine hooked to her father. A sink with a square foot of formica counter to the side of it and a cabinet above. The two of them and him. Jessica looks out the window. An airplane is flying by in the distance. Closer there is a gray-and-white gull dipping and rising slightly, like a pulse, not moving forward at all, revealing that outside it is windy.

Jessica says, "What's going to happen to him?"

"That's the difficult thing about comas. He could stay like this for a day or for fifteen years."

"There's nothing to do?"

"Monitoring, of course. . . . Minor adjustments to his care. . . . Unless he had a health-care directive of some kind suggesting he wanted it otherwise. A withdrawal of care. . . . Less than extraordinary measures. . . ."

Jessica shakes her head. "Not that I know of."

The doctor looks tactfully at the floor.

Jessica says, "Can I ask . . . Is he getting everything he needs? I mean, I don't know what kind of insurance he has. . . ."

"For a condition like this there aren't really any choices at this stage. We do the same for everyone."

"So there isn't anything I can do to help?"

The doctor's eyelids flutter the way they do when people know more about you than they should. "In a few weeks if there's been no change we'll get ready to transfer him to a long-term-care facility, and those vary in quality. I could have our care coordinator call you about that. About where you want him to go."

Jessica shakes her head miserably. She doesn't even try to hide it anymore. She wipes under her eyes with the heels of both hands.

Dr. Stern pulls a trifolded pamphlet from his pocket, and Jessica accepts it. Blurred to black-and-gray in the background is a photograph of the face of a smiling elderly woman and over it in big bright yellow letters is the title: "Reaching Out for the Help You Need."

Jessica blushes crimson, her heart beating wildly. She keeps her head bowed, studying it and waiting, certain that there is some kind of witchcraft at work; that Dr. Stern has seen inside her and that this offering is prelude to an oracular judgment and prophecy of the most grave and personal kind.

But instead he says gently, "There's a phone number on the back. They can refer you to counseling groups for people in your situation. . . ."

And Jessica looks up finally—sunglassless, hatless, tearstained. The confusion and incredulity she feels must be all over her face, because the doctor's eyes flutter again. "Families of coma patients, I mean."

Jessica flips over the pamphlet: "National Family Caregivers Association, Kensington, Maryland."

The doctor brings his fist to his mouth and clears his throat. "We try to limit visit length in the ICU, but I'm going to extend yours."

Jessica goes on staring down at the pamphlet.

He adds, "There's quite a bit of research that indicates coma patients can hear and process language, recognize voices," and when he slips out of the room he closes the door with almost no sound.

Jessica makes herself look at her father then, and she thinks about what the doctor said. His eyelids are wrinkled like crepe paper. The circlets of bandaid rise and fall with his breathing. She could say anything, deliver any rebuttal, and he would hear it and he would neither be able to respond nor to deliver a tape of her words to a tabloid to be cut and twisted in misleading ways. She can in fact declare anything—that he's been wrong about her, and that the way he has profited from betraying her is also wrong. That she is a good daughter, a good wife and mother, a good person. That she is simply good. And she finds that although she can imagine the words she might use, without his skepticism to fight she is able to see for the first time that she herself does not believe them. It occurs to her finally in a rush of panic and discouragement that all these years she has been running from the wrong things. For here she is—her father can say nothing to confuse her and every single stranger she has encountered on this trip beyond the safety of her Beverly Hills gate has been unfailingly kind. She has no critics, and still she feels ashamed.

She pulls out her cell phone. She presses one button and raises it to her ear.

"How's it going?" Akhil says.

"He's in a coma."

"What?"

"It wasn't a setup. He's been unconscious for two weeks."

She's crying again.

He lets her do this for thirty seconds or so. Then he says, "How do you feel about that?"

"At first I was pissed off, actually, because I didn't get to do what I came for."

"What was that again?"

"Seize the sword. Call his bullshit. Tell him I know I'm a good daughter no matter what he gets the tabloids to say. And then I—"

"What?"

"It's so terrible."

"What?"

"And then I thought—I really thought this, that's how despicable I am—I thought, finally I can be in a room with him without worrying about him hurting me."

"That's not despicable, it's compassionate."

"I even put chapstick on him," she says miserably. "I used his coma-tose body to play house: good daughter with sick father."

"It's compassionate that you want to visit him and take care of him after what he's done."

She shrugs, although he can't see it. Then she says, "His dog bit me."

"What? Where?"

"On the hand. Don't worry, I got it treated. The doctor said to tell you she graduated with honors from Johns Hopkins."

"Was the dog vaccinated?"

"By my dad? Who knows? But the doctor said the odds of rabies are extremely low anyway, and then with the way Grace is acting, almost nil. Does that sound right?"

"Were you offering her food?"

"Yes! That's what she asked me. And Dana too. Since when is care-taking such a risk factor?! But yes, and she's deaf and blind now she's so old. She was just confused."

"She's right, then, you don't need to worry. We should watch the dog for ten days here at home though."

"Yes, yes, I know. But I can't."

"Why not?"

"I can't bring home a dog that gets confused when you give her treats and sometimes attacks. How would it even work?! We'd have her in a fenced area of some sort where the girls could see her but not touch her, and they'd build up some fantasy in their minds about what it would be like if they talked me out of it and I let us keep her at the end of the ten days, and then what? I disappoint them and pack her into the car and take her where? Who's going to adopt a dog that bites people who feed her? A dog who's about to die anyway?"

"You could euthanize her now."

She laughs, a weird, bitter laugh with a bit of spittle.

"What?" he says.

"I seem to be killing off inconvenient loved ones right and left here. Euthanize my childhood puppy. Grateful for my father's coma. What a discovery! Permanent unconsciousness for all my difficult charges!"

"Jess—"

"If only we could get the dog into a coma, then everything would be perfect! No worries about her hurting anyone and I wouldn't have to make any decisions—"

"Sweetie—"

"Maybe when one of our girls goes through a rebellious teen stage we can put her in a coma, too."

"Jessica, wait—"

"Watch out! Watch out! Don't cheat on me or I might be hoping for a coma for you, too. So much easier to explain to the children than a divorce. So much less complicated."

"You're not being fair to yourself at all."

She shakes her head and covers her mouth with her hand, crying silently.

He says, "And I could never in a million years cheat on you. Not even if you daydreamed about inducing my coma."

She squeezes her eyes shut. She feels a flash of jealous anger. For him this would all be so simple. Kill the dog. Forget the con-man father. Welcome home his sad, lost, crazy wife. *Can I be the first one to hug you?*

"Sweetheart?"

She opens her eyes and looks at her dad. At his tubes and his brittle dyed hair.

"Jess, are you still there?"

She sniffs and wipes the snot from her nose with the back of her wrist.

He says, "Have you thought about calling anyone for help with all this?"

"What do you think I'm doing here?"

"I mean—anyone else?"

She looks out the window. The gull is back, but farther from the window, rising and falling, rising and falling in that same place.

Akhil says, "You know—someone who might have experience that could help you? With your dad or with dogs?"

"Don't you dare!" she snaps. "Don't you dare mix her into this."

"I just—"

"This isn't about her!"

"Okay—"

"We're going to leave her right where she asked to be left!"

"I just—"

"Don't try to fix me, Akhil. Don't get out your trauma flow sheet. Don't start eyeing me for secondary and tertiary conditions."

"Forget it. Forget I said that—"

Her mittened hand floats, shaking crazily, to her forehead. "This trip is over. The hospital has my number, and they're going to call me before they make any changes. I'm going to go to my car. I'm going to e-mail Larry and ask him to set up a quarantine kennel for my angry dog somewhere the girls can't see her. I'm going to go get some Chinese food. I'm going to eat it on my bed in my motel room and watch Pay Per View until I fall asleep. Then I'm coming home."

9

Long Nights

It is dusk outside the hospital, and Dana is still waiting for the message from Velasquez. What she will do when she gets it is easy for her—it will take minutes; she has done it a hundred times before. What she dreads is what will happen afterward, when she is alone in her motel room, and there is no excuse not to call Ian and tell him what she knows. He will want something from her she cannot give him. He will be hoping she is on the fence, but she is never on the fence. He will be hoping she is just afraid, but she is never afraid. He will be hoping she is full of hidden feeling, and instead, mostly, she feels nothing. Dana is a woman who always knows what she wants, and although at first people like this, later (she knows; has learned this in the handful of times she has tried to get close to people) they do not. Dana is going to get an abortion, and it is going to disappoint him, and she is going to miss him when he is gone.

Because her work now is helped by looking at her BlackBerry, making the boy wonder what tips she is reading, she continues to use the time to prepare. If she is going to lose Ian (and she knows she will now, as she has always guessed she would), she can at least help him. She can protect him a bit. She can do the things for him she is actually well designed to do.

She opens another file:

It is not unusual for some claims to be denied or for insurers to say they will not cover a test, procedure, or service that doctors order. If this happens, it is important to have a relationship with a customer service representative or case manager with whom you can talk about the situation.

Ian has said he will appeal, but she guesses he has not yet done so because he believes (some people really believe this) that something good may happen to him without his effort or planning. She guesses that although he says he has taken action, he has not done research or written a letter. Dana understands that outside her office and other small pockets of the world like it, few people ever do these things, while Dana herself always does them. She cannot skip these steps. She can never not do them. She would have liked to be able to give Ian the letter she will draft before she tells him about her pregnancy and her abortion, but she has modified her plan. She will give him her appeal advice over the phone, and she will wait for him to absorb it. She will draw the moment out, reading the letter slowly, letting him interrupt with comments, likely something unreasonable and surprising that will make her heart lift. Then she will tell him about the abortion.

He will be amazed. He will say things like "Is that it?" (people often say things like this to Dana, as if word volume were a meter for depth of feeling; as if confusion and evasion and the inability to express oneself succinctly were correlated with capacity for love), and her failure to think of more words to say will add to his dawning feeling that she is cold. And then he will forget all about the appeal letter that might help him get treatment for his cancer. To guard against this possibility, Dana will deliver a thumb drive containing the letter when she gets home. She can fit it beneath his door in a Tyvek envelope so that fruit and wet birdseed hulls do not damage the drive. He will find it when it crinkles beneath his bare feet, and however he feels when he sees it, ultimately he will open it because he is curious. Most people are at least curious. And then it may still do some good. This is Dana's plan. She will follow it to the letter. It is the best she can do.

Now a text pops up on her screen, this one from Velasquez:

> Finished at location 2. Exiting within view of your current position in 2–3 minutes.

And Dana stands, and the boy looks up at her. She slips her Black-Berry in her back pocket and slings her camera strap around her neck, not meeting his eyes. The light all around them is gray, but for the city in the distance casting its lurid yellow glow on the sky, obscuring any sunset. She grabs her backpack and heads for the automatic doors.

It is as easy as she expected it to be.

She is not inside a full thirty seconds before the boy shows up behind her. She is already at the registration desk, smiling politely at a sour-faced gatekeeper with plucked eyebrows raised above her reading glasses and her chin lowered in disapproval.

"I have an appointment with Dr. Lamb," Dana says.

"Well, I'll need your name first, dear."

"Dana Bowman."

The woman squints and clicks away skeptically on her keyboard and then pauses for it to respond. She asks for Dana's ID and examines it closely and then slides a clipboard across the counter. "Sign in here, and then head to second-floor registration. You'll need to check in there as well."

"Thanks," she says, and she glides along to the elevators, leaving the boy behind. Like every good warrior Dana knows there are so many barriers in the world—doors, gates, officious receptionists, rivers, angry dogs, bouncers. If you only know how to position yourself on the opposite side of them you can conserve so much energy; there is so little need to fight.

"I'm headed to the second floor too," he says.

"I'll need you to sign in first," the woman says.

"But I just want to visit someone."

"Well, I need to know whom, young man," she says, making herself taller in the chair. "And I'll need your name as well."

And then the elevator doors slide shut.

Alone inside, Dana removes the hour's disguise. She takes the lens cap from her pocket and snaps it on. She removes her camera and puts it gently in her backpack. She takes out her shirt and buttons it on over her tank top. She takes a tissue from a neat little plastic dispenser and wipes off the black lipstick as the door slides open on two, and then she walks down a long hallway toward the stairwell, past the ICU waiting area where paper cups litter the side tables and half a dozen people are thumbing their phone keys and flipping through magazines alone and waiting for the sick and fragile people they love, and she hustles down, hustles down, a plainer version of herself, neutral, not sexy or distracting, her usual costume of inscrutability, her easiest one.

Outside in the parking lot, there is a bird chirping in a tree, and one motor idling in the distance. Dana knows that minutes ago Velasquez and Jessica passed the bench where the boy had been sitting, escaping the hospital unnoticed to get in their cars and drive to the motel as planned. She will not see them tonight unless something goes wrong. Already she is alone again. Already it is almost time for her to lose him. Only the dog stands between her and the tasks that will bring her to that loss.

She strides across the lot, and as she approaches the dark Suburban, she can hear Grace whining—a long high squeak punctuated by pauses at random intervals for her to return to feverish panting. Although Dana cracked the front windows for air, the glass is so cloudy with the dog's condensed breath that she has to wipe the inside of her windshield with a towel before she can even see. She drives with a map marked "Hospital to Motel" on the seat beside her, her jaw set as Grace continues to keen behind her, and she follows its bullet-pointed instructions to a stucco building thinly reminiscent of a mission, with a bell at the top and an incongruous set of automatic sliding glass doors at the front. She rolls the windows up and grabs her backpack and the empty Petco bag and gets out of the car, shutting her door, freeing herself for just a moment from the manic sound of the dog. It is replaced by the happy sounds of splashing and calling from a swimming pool she cannot see and will not go to investigate. Her task tonight is clear: (1) be available for emergencies; (2) be well rested for duty tomorrow; (3) care for the dog.

When she opens the tailgate, there is Grace—big and blind, tied and muzzled. Her water bowl is empty, but the carpeted floor around her is soaked, and she is panting so hard and fast it is like the sound of someone scratching at a wall, an endless frantic repetitive clicking, like panic itself. The breeze gets her attention, and she turns her muzzle toward the open door and skitters her feet as much as her tether will allow. Dana picks up the overturned bowl and puts it in the thin plastic bag and loops this over her wrist. Then she unties the leash and lifts her, whimpering and thrashing, and sets her on the asphalt before her. And Grace keeps whining, even when she pauses in her own shambling to pee, not crouching, just letting her waters dribble out onto her long shadow on the blacktop, and run back toward the wheel of Dana's armored car.

Dana has, as she told Ian, always loved motels, but her passage through a side door into this one is not the comfort it has always been. Grace's nails make a ripping sound on the hallway rug—a nubby brown industrial carpet with an acrid plasticky smell—and the fluorescent lights tremor slightly in a way that makes the hallway pulse. Theirs is the first door, and when Dana opens it and flips on the lights, right away the dog begins growling. Dana has to nudge her a little and tug at the leash to get her to cross the threshold, and when she tries to close the door she has to grasp Grace's tail to keep it from getting caught in the jamb. Then the dog stumbles and throws her weight against the door, slamming it shut, and when Dana releases her leash, Grace stays there, pressing her haunches up against the door in the corner and digging her nails deep into the carpet.

Dana adjusts her plan for the night. There will be her conversation with Ian, but there will also be the till-and-plow work of caregiving tasks

and unthreatening gestures she undertakes to soften Grace to her surroundings so that ultimately, sometime, perhaps close to midnight, the
dog can stop whining long enough for the two of them to sleep. Beyond
all evidence and reason, Dana does still from day to day hope for the
ability to sleep.

Step one is water. She flips on the harsh white light of the bathroom.
She pulls the beveled plastic sink knob and fills one metal bowl and then
sets it on the floor of the bathroom to minimize the mess. Right away,
though, she sees that for now at least it is hopeless. Grace is still cower-
ing by the door to the room, folded up on the threshold in a cartoonish
way, in a small contorted shape it is hard to believe her big body can
even make. Dana steps into her room and sets her heavy backpack on
the bed, making a crater in the center of the polyester spread reminiscent
of models of gravity fields. If you set something along the bed's edge—a
marble, or a dinner roll, or even an infant—it would roll inexorably
toward Dana's densely packed backpack.

Then Dana begins. She takes out her BlackBerry and types this message to Ian:

> In my motel room. I can talk anytime now. Call or text when
> you're ready.

And she reaches across the perfect gravity-scape of the bed, and from
an outer compartment in her backpack she withdraws a thin laptop and
a file of sample insurance letters. The backpack wobbles a bit on the
soft mattress and resettles, its zippered compartment of stiff black ballistic nylon hanging open like a door or a mouth. She looks around the
room. Navy and red and brown, with a dark peeling presswood dresser
topped by a television with wood veneer siding and shiny chrome knobs
you have to twist. Above the bed there is no picture, only a blank wall.
Dana decides to sit not on the bed but in a wood-framed armchair in the
corner where she can see both the door and the dog. She takes out the
folder and opens it, and the letter she took from Ian's kitchen is on top,

a phone number in crayon scrawled next to the stick figure with arms embracing rays of light.

She opens her laptop.

While she works, Grace alternates between growling and that panicky high-pitched rhythmic whine she began in the car, and she is still standing with one whole side of her body leaning against the door. It is such a strange and difficult posture to maintain that from time to time her muscles seem to spasm, and she pauses in her growling and slips and repositions herself with a surprisingly loud scrabble of her collar metal against the door. Dana presses on, drafting her letter, tapping out with a blank face phrases like, "in reference to your letter," and "copies of any expert medical opinions," and "treating physician may respond to its applicability to," ignoring the growl and scrape, growl and scrape, until she hears a banging on the wall.

It comes from just behind the bed that bears her backpack.

Not a headboard knocking. Not a hammer nailing.

A fist pounding.

A neighbor complaining about the noise of the dog.

Dana thinks about her options. It is, after all, a motel that accepts pets. The dog's growl and collar scrape is no louder than a television at regular volume, but perhaps more annoying because it is intermittent. She turns the television on and flips through the channels—news, cell phone commercial, cartoons—and picks something fairly loud, something with a car chase, but leaves it at polite volume. Grace does not even flinch at the sound, but when Dana crosses the room to set a treat on the floor at the dog's feet, the growl deepens and the fur between her shoulder blades stands on end. Dana retreats, past the strangely forbidding gravity field of her backpack, and settles again in the straight-backed chair.

She types "please furnish the credentials" and "essential treatment." She makes use of boldface and italics. She paragraphs frequently. She clarifies antecedents. She divides independent clauses into two sentences, and backs up frequently, saving and resaving the file, IanAppeal.doc, and then rereading it again and editing further until she has eliminated all traces of ambiguity and emotion, has spell- and grammar-checked, has compared and reverified the mailing address against the paper copy she took from him, and then she opens a small pocket inside her backpack and withdraws a tiny blue thumb drive.

The dog does not lie down, but she does change from growling again to that strange keening noise, a squeak with each quick shallow breath. She is almost hyperventilating, and Dana is glancing at the clock on the nightstand so frequently (8:20, 8:25, 8:45) that when there is a knock at the door it is synchronized with one of these glances, as if her preoccupation with time itself has caused it.

Dana stands and checks the gun in her ankle holster, and then she steps to the vestibule. She has to lean over the growling dog to peer through the eyehole. A heavyset man in a bathrobe. Empty hands. Big loose pockets, though. No shoes.

She reaches down and pulls Grace as gently as she can by the collar, making her spring up wildly, banging her head clumsily against the door and resetting her claws in the carpet. Dana opens the door against the brass security latch and looks at her visitor through the crack. He looks down toward the sound of the growling, but he cannot see the captive Grace behind Dana's door.

He wrinkles his brow. "Um, I'm sorry to bother you."

Dana blinks.

"It's about your dog," he says, his eyes flicking down again. "The noise it's making."

"My apologies," Dana says.

He has a sweaty forehead, and his eyes shift to the side now, down the hall. His lips are chapped, and his cheeks are red.

"I know this place takes pets. I would never complain about noise on my own so early in the evening, but my wife is—"

Grace hurls herself against the door at the man then, and it slams shut.

Dana muscles it back open.

The man's eyes are wide and startled.

Dana talks over Grace's high thin whine. "Sorry about that. And I apologize that you even had to—"

He says, "Not at all. It's early. It's just that my wife is—"

From the hall Dana hears a woman's voice now. "Tell her we'll call the front desk, Norman! Tell her we'll file a formal complaint!"

"Janice, please," the man says. And then to Dana: "I'm so sorry."

"Not at all." Dana smiles mildly. Her face is relaxed and unthreatening, a reflex from years of duties with protectees who need her to appear nonconfrontational, helpful, and unmemorable—to draw as little attention to them as possible. "You shouldn't even have to ask."

From her invisible place in the hall, the woman says, "Is she here with that dog group? Why did you book us a motel that takes pets?"

The man says, "Please, Janice." Then: "Again, I'm sorry to make such a big deal."

Dana says, "Really, it's no problem. I'll take care of it."

She closes the door, and Grace skitters again up against it.

Dana knows what to do. Although she has sedatives in her backpack she could easily adjust for an animal, she will not use them. It is one of her tasks to take good care of the dog. She empties the water bowl into the toilet and flushes it. She returns her laptop and files to her backpack and removes it from the spongy bed, leaving behind a trace of it, an impression that will disappear slowly, over minutes or even hours, but be gone before any new guests check in to the room, so that the only trace of her brief visit here will be the smell of the dog she could not calm.

Getting the door open and the dog out into the hall is an effort that involves more of that ripping noise, and more of that whining, but when they get out into the open air, the dog relaxes against the leash so suddenly that Dana stumbles. The sky is an oily blue, as dark as it will ever get in the skirtings of Las Vegas; there will never be any stars. And the birds have disappeared altogether. The air outside is still and silent. She lets Grace lead her a few yards' distance from the motel to a thin strip of grass that runs around the perimeter of the parking lot, where Grace pauses again between a lamppost and a gold Lincoln Town Car and releases more of her pee, but there is not much of it, and in the grass it makes no sound. On the dashboard of the Town Car is a box of saltines.

Dana sets a metal bowl on the grass and reaches into the backpack Ian loves (Ian, who sleeps open-armed without covers in the center of the bed) and withdraws a bottle of drinking water. She pours it into the bowl, and Grace drinks long and messily under the smeary, starless night sky, making splashing and gurgling sounds and soaking her front paws. Then Dana takes out a little camp can opener and mixes food into the remaining water with her spoon, making a thin slurry the dog can drink through the basket muzzle, and Grace drinks this too and lies down then on the grass, as if to sleep.

Dana pulls the BlackBerry from her pocket. All around them are the dark silhouettes of nursery saplings whose leaves must be spring green and whose branches must be full of the birds they can no longer see. It is 9:05. She types a message to Velasquez:

> Relocating to car for night. Dog noise in motel room disturbing adjacent guest. Use cell phone/text for communication.

Grace is making a sighing sound, and the air smells of meat, but Dana does not want her to fall asleep here in the open, where both of them will start at the comings and goings of cars and motel guests and birds. She wants to be alone in her armored car where she can lock the doors and, although the chance is of course slim, there is at least the possibility of drifting off. Maybe for a few moments here and there. She has her eye mask in her backpack. She has her sleep app. She has her white noise.

Dana tugs on the leash, and Grace resists, keeping her head low in the grass. Dana takes a bacon treat from the foil pouch and puts it in front of her nose to lead her, but she does not stir, and when Dana pulls again, she begins to growl. She decides for the moment to leave the bowls behind. She puts both arms through her backpack straps, and with both hands on the leash Dana drags her, skritching and resisting, growling and thrashing, across the pavement to the dark car and opens the tailgate. She lifts Grace into the car and the dog explodes, kicking and bucking against the walls of the car, and her tail thrashes out first on the right, then on the left. Dana pauses, watching in wonder. She tries to imagine the steps she might go through to even get the tailgate closed without risk of slamming it on the dog's tail. She could circle around to the middle row and tie Grace's leash to the handle on the back of one of the front seats, but in the few seconds it takes her to get there, Grace might fall out onto the pavement and run away. She could run away, and Dana could lose her. She could lose what she has been entrusted to protect altogether.

No. She will have to go in through the back past Grace herself, so that she can keep hold of her tether, and this is what she does. She takes off her backpack to make herself smaller. Then she threads the needle of space to the left of the bucking dog, and Grace knocks her to the side as she goes, slamming her into the windows, and Dana squeezes past and ties the leash to the handle on the back of the passenger seat. She cinches it tighter, drawing Grace farther into the car. She double-knots it, and it is then that Grace begins howling.

Really howling. The first of this noise we have heard. Dana jumps out of the car as if scalded to slam the rear door before anyone can come out to complain about the racket. Grace's tail is well in, and her paws are hiked up on the rear by the short tether at her neck, and Dana slams it, muffling and containing the noise.

She can still hear it, though. Nothing anyone else will complain about, but it is clear this arrangement will not work. Already the windows are clouding with the dog's condensed breath, and there will be no calming her inside the car. There will be no sleeping. She takes her Black-Berry from her pocket: 9:40. Still no text or missed calls. Dana braces herself. She puts her backpack back on.

As soon as Grace is back out in the open air, she eases again. She lets herself be led, padding gently, not tugging at the leash, across the pavement toward the strip of grass where Dana left the dog bowls, and she settles right away into the meat-scented grass next to the gold sedan. Dana ties her leash to the lamppost securely, a double-constrictor hitch with a slip for morning, and by the time she is finished she sees, to her utter wonder and relief, that Grace has fallen asleep.

There may be no sleep for Dana in the open, but at least she can finish her work. She can get comfortable at least. She takes out her laptop and sets her backpack next to the gold sedan and lies back against it as if it were a pillow. She checks the gun in the holster on her boot. She checks her BlackBerry again in her pocket. Then she opens the lid of her laptop. The glow from the screen lights the darkened wheel wells and the fur on Grace's snout inside the basket muzzle.

Dana rereads what she has:

> As you know, Ian Freeman was diagnosed . . . Currently Dr. Ashcroft believes . . . Enclosed please find additional information documenting . . .

And almost as quickly as the dog, she falls asleep.

She sleeps more soundly than she ever does in her own bed, and when she wakes in the grass beneath the flat sky it is not to the noise of Grace (the dog remains sleeping) but instead to the sound of a man talking to his wife.

"Easy does it. Easy there. Easy, love."

Dana sits up. She can see nothing of the parking lot from this low behind the gold sedan. There is only the dog, and the lamppost and the sky, and beyond them an anguished wail from the woman the man is coaxing: "You're not listening to me!"

"I've got you. Almost there now."

"I need to go to the bathroom, I said!"

Something clicks then in the gold sedan: the sound of doors unlocking.

Dana stands to see a woman doubled over in a nightgown, and guiding her by the elbow and shoulder is the man who knocked on Dana's door to talk to her about Grace. When the woman straightens, Dana sees that she is enormous beneath her crossed arms, and her nightgown is soaked to transparency between her legs.

Dana picks up her backpack and steps over the sleeping dog. When she steps into the lamplight in front of his car, the man sees her.

"You?"

The woman says, "Who is she, Norman?"

"She's the woman with the dog."

"I'm a paramedic," Dana says. "How far along is her pregnancy?"

"She isn't due for two weeks yet! Our niece is getting married; we thought we could go if we drove."

The woman says, "Why are you talking to her?! I need to go inside." Then she folds and moans again.

Dana says, "That's two contractions in a minute. Have you called an ambulance?"

"I was going to drive her to the hospital."

"Just take me inside, Norman. I'll be fast. I really need to go."

Dana says, "Ma'am. If the contractions are that close together, and you feel a strong need to have a bowel movement, you are going to have your baby in that bathroom. I can deliver it here in the car and get you set up to drive safely to the hospital if you'll let me."

The man reaches down under the woman and picks her up beneath the seat of her sodden nightgown, and the woman screams.

Dana opens the rear door of his gold sedan.

"Lay her down there on the seat," she says. "Then take off your pajama top for me."

"What?"

"I need something to cover the baby with." Dana opens her backpack and takes out her little bottle of hand sanitizer. She squirts it along her forearms, and it glistens under the parking lot lights. She spreads it around, rubbing it, while the man lays his wife gently on the back bench and begins unbuttoning his shirt.

From inside the car the woman says, "Remember the sounds her dog was making, Norman?! It was horrible. Why do you trust her? You're making a mistake."

"Ma'am, I'm sorry I disturbed you. I am. But I can help you if you let me. Do you know if your baby is a boy or a girl?"

The woman screams, drawing her legs up.

The man raises his hands to his head, wincing, and says, "They think it's a girl."

"Okay." She raises her voice over the woman's moan. "Ma'am, I'm going to ask your husband to take your underpants off. I'm also going to ask him to unbutton the top of your nightgown, so I can lay your little girl right on your skin when she comes out."

The husband reaches into the car and pulls the woman's underpants down. She starts to scream again, and he leans over and whispers something in her ear then as he unbuttons the front of her nightgown, and the woman stills and (there's no mistaking it) laughs softly before she begins to cry. He stands up and takes off his shirt and tries to hand it to Dana.

"If you'd hold that a minute," she says, "I'll let you know when I need it."

Then Dana kneels. The leather-covered armrest on the door presses against her side, and she can feel the grit of the asphalt through the knees of her pants.

"Okay," she says. "This is going to be easy. There are no mistakes you can make. I can see the top of your little girl's head, and I'm going to put my hand right here to support it as it comes out. When you feel the next contraction, you'll feel like pushing, and you just go ahead and push. She's going to come right out easy."

The woman screams again with the next push, and the baby's head starts to turn, and Dana can see the eyes, squeezed tight shut, and the damp red nose, and the mouth, and she takes her left hand and sweeps it under the nostrils to clear them, and then there are shoulders for her to hold, and a bottom too, and she puts her hand underneath and stands a little, squatting, to set the baby on the bare space on the woman's chest. She looks over her shoulder and reaches out a hand then, and the husband gives her his shirt, warm and flannel, which seems just right to Dana, and she wraps it around the back of the baby and begins to rub. The second stroke does the trick, and the baby wails once and coughs, and Dana can't see her little face, but she doesn't need to.

"She's okay," she says. "She's good. Your little girl is fine."

Behind the sound of the baby's cries now, and the sound of the mother crying a little, there are no other sounds. The dog is still sleeping.

She turns to the man. In the parking lot lights his bare chest is very white. She says, "Now all you have to do is drive her. She'll be fine. Don't worry about the cord. They'll take care of it at the hospital, which isn't far from here. They'll clean the baby and take care of your wife."

"I don't know what to say."

"You should probably get going. Do you know how to get there?"

"I have no idea."

She opens her backpack and looks at the little tabs she made. "Motel to Hospital" one of them says. She removes it and hands the directions to the man.

"How on earth . . . ?" he says.

"The Emergency Room is at the south end of the parking lot. That's where you should go. I'll call ahead to let them know what I've done."

"Do you have a card? So I can get in touch with you to thank you?"

"That's not necessary," she says. "You should really get going."

But he is fumbling in the pocket of his pajama pants.

"If I give you my card, will you contact me then? So we can at least send you a picture of the baby?"

He looks almost desperate, and Dana knows accepting the card will make him go. "Sure," she says.

The wallet he withdraws is black leather, and stuffed so full of cards and bills and little chits of things that he has to thumb the edges clumsily for several seconds before he gets one free. Beside them in the open car, the baby and the woman are still crying together; the woman has tucked her bloody legs in and under, making a sort of nest. Dana shuts the car door gently and accepts his card without looking at it.

"Congratulations," she says, and he gets in the car and closes his door. She dials the hospital on her BlackBerry and watches him pull back, revealing Grace still sleeping peacefully in the strip of grass by the lamppost. She asks for the Emergency Room, and then she waits a moment, looking at the dog under the blank, flat sky, almost the color of a moth wing now. Dawn is breaking. Grace is so still, Dana wonders briefly if she has died in her sleep.

Then she hears the ER operator on the phone.

Dana says, "I'm an EMT from Los Angeles County and I delivered a baby in a car five minutes from you. They are on their way to you now. Mother and baby are both fine. Umbilical cord still attached, uncut."

"Name?"

Dana looks away from the dog, at the card. The card is very white, and on it is a little blue figure with upraised arms filled with rays of yellow light and this: NORMAN REITMAN, SENIOR CLAIMS EXAMINER, AETNA INSURANCE.

The sky is lightening now. Along the horizon over the eastern hills is a thin limn of red, and then a pale haze just above it. The air around her is gray and thick with moisture. The operator asks her again for the name and Dana gives it to him, and then he thanks her, and she hangs up, and right away her phone beeps to indicate a new voice mail waiting, one from Ian that she listens to there in the misty parking lot next to Jessica's sleeping dog.

"Dana! I just got your message. I stayed at the wedding till everyone was gone, and then I stayed up in the lobby talking to Darius and Leslie all night, and they're driving me home right now. We're on La Cienega. I would love to talk to you about anything! Call me!"

Dana breathes out and in sharply—a sort of laugh—and she covers her mouth with a hand still smeared with blood.

When she dials him back she can hear her own heart beating, a pulse in her ears speeding up with each ring, but he doesn't answer. She gets his voice mail finally: "This is Ian; leave your number so I don't have to clean my apartment to find it."

"Ian!" she says. "I don't know how I missed you, you just called me!" Her voice is shaky. "Shit." She laughs at herself and rubs a bloody hand through her hair. "I don't know what to say. Just call me," she says, and she presses a button.

She kneels in the space where the gold sedan had been and repacks her backpack then. She puts her hand sanitizer away and draws out the ziplock bag of ziplock bags and puts the card inside one. To be safe she thumbs her code into her BlackBerry and opens her contacts and types the name in, and the phone number too, and double-checks it and saves it and also e-mails it to herself before secreting the card in the bag in the pocket of her backpack. There is a new text from Velasquez now: "Principal requesting departure in ten minutes. You ready?"

"Ready," Dana types.

When Dana goes to the lobby bathroom to wash up, she takes Grace with her. The dog stirs at the smell of Dana's boots beside her in the grass, but does not startle, just stands up slowly, as if her joints hurt a little, and then follows easily, across the lot, through the automatic doors, past the pump carafes in the coffee-scented lobby, and into a white-and-black room where they are once again alone. Grace sits patiently while Dana washes her hands first, and her forearms too, soaping generously, up to a frothy bubble. Her hair is damp with sweat, and she splashes her face to clean it and looks at herself in the mirror, blinking. She shakes her head. Then she goes into the bigger bathroom stall, the handicapped, so that Grace can fit in there with her, and she sets the leash and her backpack on the floor, and Grace lies down as she had in the parking lot grass, a white shape breaking up the pattern of tiles on the floor, a pattern of triangles, black and white, like the tiles in the print above her bed that turn, row by row, into birds. Dana stares at the tiles, her clean hands on the waistband of her pants, ready to unbutton them but hesitating. She laughs again, the same short airy laugh of surprise at herself she laughed during her disjointed message to Ian, someone else's voice really, and then she unbuttons her pants and pulls them down, crouching to sit, until she sees the blood.

It is not a huge amount, but of course, it does not have to be for Dana to understand what has happened. She sits down on the hard white seat and stares at it, peeing, an almost musical sound, and when she is done, she goes on sitting. Two or three minutes pass, and Dana holds perfectly still, her boots on the triangle tiles and her pants bunched around the gun still hidden underneath on her boot, staring at this smear of blood in her underpants, her face a dull nothing. Finally she opens a zipper pouch in her backpack and withdraws two ziplock bags—one full of panty liners and the other of tampons, and she takes care of things briskly, and flushes, and zips the pack and washes again, and without looking again at her face in the mirror, she walks out into the parking lot.

Where it is dawn finally, the sky pale, but light enough to cast dim shadows—the long T of the Holiday Inn sign on the asphalt.

She goes to her car, and sees that Jessica and Velasquez are just crossing the blacktop with their overnight bags. Jessica's eyelids are puffy, and her lips are chapped. She steps forward and smiles at Dana in her nervous way. "How is Grace this morning?"

"She seems to be fine, ma'am."

"Did she keep you up?" The question makes her blush.

"Not at all. She slept right through."

"We should let her walk before we go, then," Jessica says. "I'll do it. I'd like to. My hand feels much better this morning. It doesn't hurt so much anymore."

"Certainly." Dana hands her Grace's leash, and despite what she claimed, Jessica takes it with her left hand. She leads her dog haltingly toward the open field beside the hotel—a field of grasses.

Dana is alone with Velasquez.

"So," she says, "what's the plan?"

"Head back to L.A. She wants help quarantining the dog out of sight at home. I called ahead to Larry. We're thinking of the greenhouse storeroom. It has a concrete floor with a drain."

They are not looking at each other but out over the field, where Jessica is knee-deep in grasses and the dog's head is just visible. She is walking quickly, and at the same time, because some critical distance has been breached, both Velasquez and Dana begin walking to close the space between them. The dog and Jessica are speeding up now, the dog's leash is taut, and Jessica's arm is stretched out in front of her, the dog clearly pulling for something, and Dana and Velasquez break out in a run. They are nearing the far end of the field, where a wood-and-wire fence marks the boundary of the motel property, and the dog stumbles often in the grass because she cannot see the things hidden beneath, nor can she see the barbed-wire fence as she nears it and runs right into it, tearing open the white fur at her neck.

Day 3

10

Difficult Conversations

Lynn stands in her kitchen squinching her eyes shut tight, patting a screaming baby slung over her shoulder—the boy, tiny in a blue T-shirt and diaper. The baby girl is in her carrier, the one on the scarred wood table, also screaming, and on the counter are two dirty bottle feeders, their milky clouded plastic liners squeezed empty. Lynn pats the wailing boy's back and looks at the screaming girl. She says, "I'm coming for you," but it is hopeless. There is no picking up the girl with the handle of the carrier in the way, and anyway what would she do with the baby she has? How does Vivian do it? To Lynn the little girl looks stockaded. She lowers a hand to feel along the sides of the handle—"How on earth?"— and leans sideways as far as she can without dropping the boy to see if there is something—a handle? a button? a lever? What would it be?—to free this little girl from the safety seat where she lies crying.

Then the phone starts to ring.

"Crap," she says. "Crap, crap, crap."

She keeps searching along the sides of Emmaline's carrier, ignoring each ring, which mixes in anyhow with the louder racket of the babies' screaming. She cups the little girl's hot red cheek, and in the voice she reserves for dogs, she says, "I'm sorry, baby girl." Then she moves her hand to the back of Sebastian's head to support it while she bends over farther, hoping to see something—anything!—and finally she spots a release.

She rights herself and takes her good hand from the boy's head to squeeze a red trigger, pushing on the handle of the carrier with the elbow on her other arm, the one holding the boy, and when the handle buckles, it jostles him in her arms so suddenly and violently he windmills his arms in panic and screams even louder, but—ah! there we go!—the handle clicks out of place and down.

"There now," she says in her dog voice. "Everything is going to be fine."

The phone is still ringing, though, and when it finally stops, Lynn doesn't even seem to notice. She is staring at Emmaline, whose face is almost purple now with fury. Lynn stands right against the table and slides the carrier toward her body as she's seen Vivian do and cups her right hand under Emmaline's thigh, but instead of lifting her neatly into the crook of her arm, she only rolls on her side in the carrier, a final injustice that makes Emmaline kick and hold her breath, purpling further, so for a moment Lynn thinks the girl might never breathe again. "Come on now," she says, patting her on the arm, shaking her gently. "It's not over yet, give me a chance," while Emmaline stretches out farther and farther, like a tiny dark board of wood, and then finally—thank whoever made us!—buckles over in her safety seat to take a breath before she starts screaming again.

Lynn takes a pacifier from the pocket of her sweater and puts it in the baby girl's mouth, but the girl spits it out so forcefully it clears not just her seat but the edge of the table and bounces once on the seat of the spindle chair before clattering onto the floor. Lynn decides they both need a minute—a little breather—before trying again, and she raises the handle on the seat and hefts it off the table and begins to swing it, making a pendulum of her right arm, while in her left she still jiggles Sebastian. Both babies are still crying, and now she tries dancing a little jig. She backs through the door to the side yard, and for a blessed moment both babies stop crying, surprised by the fresh air. But they start in again soon enough, first with little whimpers, almost matching each other noise for noise, building up again to full angry wails while the dogs freeze in their tracks and cock their heads this way and that at the sound, which builds up in no time to the racket she'd been getting in the kitchen.

She looks from one to the other, blinking in wonder.

Then the phone starts ringing again.

This time Lynn takes the babies inside and sets them down, fitting Sebastian back into his safety seat. She grabs the receiver and steps alone out into the fresh and closes the door on the crying.

It is fainter now, but still clear through the open kitchen windows.

She presses a button to answer.

"Vivian?"

"No." It's a woman's voice. Lynn raises a hand to her mouth but says nothing.

There is a long pause.

The voice says, "No, Mom. It's me."

Lynn lets her hand slip down to her heart.

Jessica says, "Is that a baby crying?"

Lynn's lips tremble. Tears come to her eyes, but her voice is even. "Two, actually."

"I called at a bad time then."

"No, no—" Lynn bites her lip to steady her voice. "They'll be all right." And sure enough already something in there is slowing. Lynn peers through the window and sees that the girl is sucking her fist and the boy has caught sight of the ceiling fan.

In her car Jessica sits back and looks at the horizon. There is nothing out there, only scrub and sky. Jaya's red shoes sit beside her. She stares for a minute or more, and her mother says nothing, but the baby sound grows a little more muffled. Finally she says, "I have a favor to ask you."

Lynn swallows. Her hand is over the mouthpiece of the phone, and she is looking at the dogs. They are digging around the hose bib again— a big trough exposing the pipe. There is a five-gallon bucket of sand on a dolly in the garage, and every day she wheels it out and refills the hole. She peels back her fingers from the phone and says, "Anything."

"It's nothing big."

"Okay."

"Nothing personal. It's just a dog."

"All right."

"She's just injured and needs some stitching."

Lynn holds very still.

"Anyway, I was wondering if you could do it for me."

"Where are you?"

"Not far. A suburb of Vegas."

Tears roll down Lynn's cheek. She clears her throat. "Absolutely I can. I'll be ready for it when you get here."

When Jessica pulls in, Lynn is standing on the porch in her vinyl apron. She steps down the stairs, out of the shadow of the eave and into the sun, and watches three dark Suburbans roll down the gravel drive, and her eyes scan between them, waiting to see which of them bears her daughter. The second car pulls off to the side to let the third pass so that just two come through the neck of the driveway into the big open circle of dried mud. When the door on the lead car opens and Jessica steps out, Lynn folds her left arm beneath her chest and covers her mouth with her hand.

Jessica stands in her bloodstained sweatshirt with one hand on her open car door. Lynn takes a quick swipe under each eye with her fingers.

Twenty feet of dry earth stands between them.

Finally Jessica gestures over her shoulder with her left thumb. "She's bleeding pretty badly."

Lynn nods. "I'm ready for her," she says, and points to the dark open garage and waits to see what her daughter will do.

Neither of them moves.

It is the bridge of etiquette with a stranger that finally closes the gap between them. When Dana steps out of her Suburban and walks forward to Jessica's side, Lynn crosses the turnaround to meet her. Their three bodies make a single shadow on the ground.

Jessica says, "Mom, this is Dana. Dana, this is my mother, Lynn."

Back at the motel, holding the bleeding dog, Jessica had told Dana she would lead them to her mother's dog shelter for medical treatment, and in this simple statement a full set of possible threats and privacy issues of import made themselves as plain to Dana as pockets large enough for weapons in the folds of civilian clothes. In the security procedures log for Jessica's property, there are fifteen full pages devoted to the handling of calls or visits from her father, and not a single mention of a mother. After a count of two seconds Dana had said, "Certainly. I'll be available for any help you specify when we arrive on-site. Barring any instruction from you, would you prefer a default of body accompaniment or surveillance from a distance?" "From a distance," she'd said.

Dana shakes Lynn's hand, but she does not tell her it is a pleasure to meet her. Instead she says this: "Would now be a good time to help you two move the dog?"

Lynn blinks.

Dana doesn't wait for an answer. She leads mother and daughter silently to the back of her armored car and pops the tailgate to show them Grace waiting: white, muzzled, tethered to the tie-down by a leather lead, lying still on the bloody mat. The cut on her neck is ragged and long, and the basket muzzle is slick with her bubbly drools.

Dana takes the two corners of the tailgate mat beneath Grace's head to make a stretcher of it, and Lynn and Jessica look at the corners beneath her tail. Right away it is clear to all three of them what will need to happen. Jessica reaches in with her uninjured hand to grab the back corner, and Lynn takes the other corner with hers, each woman trying as best she can to give the other space, not quite touching, not even facing each other really, trailing the dog behind them as they face forward and lumber toward the garage and pass out of the bright light and into its cool dark concrete-scented shade. It is an awkward business, but they manage to get the dog up onto the sheet, still lying on the bloody car mat but finally there at least, on a white sheet in the sun from the window. Without saying a word Lynn picks up a needle and begins, and Dana retreats to the center of the turnaround, watching their backs from the distance Jessica had requested. Lynn's elbow rises with each long pull of the thread, and Jessica stands beside her resting her hand on the dog's flank, and neither of their heads move with talking. They are both watching the dog, Grace scrabbling a bit with each pull and her head straining toward the wall and her black lips curled inside the cage of the muzzle at the pain of mending.

When Lynn ties the knot and snips it, she steps to the sink to wash her hands. Her stitching is tight and even, the flesh mounded in places and bristling with white fur. Jessica keeps a hand on Grace's flank and watches her mother's hands at the sink, her good hand and her bad one, soaping and rinsing more than is probably needed.

Lynn turns to her when she's clean, but she doesn't say anything.

Jessica says, "Thank you."

Lynn looks at her, blinking, considering the different replies she might make.

Jessica says, "Should she rest here?"

"We should lower her to the floor. She might try to stand when we leave, and fall."

They can manage just the two of them this time, each taking two corners of the big white sheet in one hand and lifting it like a hammock and lowering it gently to the floor Vivian mopped clean the day before. Grace's eyes are closed, and her red-soaked chest rises and lowers visibly with her breaths. They stare at her as if it is needed, both of them wondering what to say.

Finally Lynn works up her courage. "Can I fix you a cup of tea?"

Jessica goes on looking at the dog. She stares at it so long Lynn thinks of asking it again, and then finally Jessica says, "I guess that would be all right."

Lynn leads the way to her kitchen, and Jessica follows. They pass in through the living room, stepping over the baby gate and crinkling past the mama dog with her puppies wrestling alongside. They pass in through the dark front hall and on into the kitchen. Lynn takes the kettle from the stove and fills it standing at the sink, the yellow-curtained windows with the mountains in the distance and the bright blue sky framing her there. Jessica lays a hand on the chair and glances at her mother's back at the sink. A pair of baby bottles and nipples sit clean in the drying rack beside her.

"Where are the babies?"

"Upstairs sleeping," her mother says without turning. "I wore them out, I guess, with my rusty handling."

"Whose are they?"

Lynn puts the kettle on the stove and lights the burner with the long-handled lighter, holding the stove knob in. It clicks a few times before it catches. She says, "They belong to a girl who's staying here and helping me out with the dogs. She needed to be gone today, and I told her I'd watch over them." She turns and faces her daughter. Jessica is picking at the gauze on her wounded hand.

Lynn says, "What happened there?"

"The dog bit it."

"Do you know if she's had her shots?"

"I don't. I got the bite checked by a doctor, though. She said it was fine and I should just keep an eye on the dog for the next ten days to make sure her behavior doesn't seem rabid."

"I could do that for you."

"Could you?"

"I'd like to."

Jessica looks down at her lap, and Lynn looks outside at her dogs still digging around the pipe. They are quiet so long the water in the kettle begins to make that hushing sound it will make before it boils.

Finally Jessica says, "It's Dad's dog."

Lynn regards her. She has never in her life felt so careful about what she might say.

Jessica says, "He's in the hospital, and his neighbors were complaining about the barking so his landlady called me."

Lynn holds very still while Jessica says this, her eyes on Jessica's face and her own face neutral. In the pause that follows she finally nods—an infinitesimal movement of her chin. Then she takes out two blue enamel cups and sets them softly on the table. And she takes out the paper box of teas and sets this there too. Then a squeeze bottle of honey shaped like a bear. She pours the water into each cup and puts the kettle back on the stove. She sits down in the second chair, across from her daughter. Jessica sifts through the bags and selects one—Apple Cinnamon—and after she withdraws her hand, without looking Lynn takes one herself—Lemon, it turns out to be. Lynn pinches the bag between her metal loops and tears with her fingers, and Jessica fumbles a moment in her lap under the table and then grips hers in her mouth and tears with her left hand.

Lynn says, "Do you need anything for it? Tylenol or Advil or anything?"

And Jessica says, "What were you calling to say all those times?"

"What?"

"What were you calling to say—all those times you tried calling me through the studio?"

Lynn swallows, the dry tea bag still in her hand. She holds it there, watching her daughter busy herself, looking down, setting her tea bag in her cup and trailing the string out onto the table; pinching the white paper tab on the end of her tea bag string and folding it.

Lynn says, "First just 'I love you and I'm sorry.' "

Jessica pleats and re-pleats the little white paper with her fingers. "Something different after that?"

"Yes. Later it was also 'I stopped drinking and I know how I hurt you. And if you're willing to hear it I'd like to list all the ways so I can make amends.' " She is looking down now, trying to stand her dry tea bag on the wood table. "It was part of my twelve-step program."

"How long ago did you stop drinking?"

"Four years and twenty-seven days."

Jessica's lips tremble and her eyes well up. She picks up her cup and takes a small sip and sets it down, looking off to the side, at the sink, or the window while her mother regards her, still not brewing her own tea. Jessica swipes under her eyes and then looks down at her tea. "That's good. That must be, I mean."

Lynn nods.

"I'm sorry I didn't let you tell me."

"I was a scary person—a person who loved you and also hurt you. That's what you knew."

She sets her tea bag on the surface of the water in her own cup finally. They both watch it darken and sink.

Lynn says, "I'd like to say it still, if it's okay with you."

Jessica's hands rise to the sides of her face, not quite covering her ears. She laughs nervously and crosses her arms and then uncrosses them, settling her hand and the big mitten of gauze together in her lap. "All right," she says.

"You sure?"

"Yes."

"Okay then." Lynn stands and reaches up onto the high shelf and behind the bottle and she withdraws the piece of lined paper, folded and folded and folded again so that it can hide there, long and thin. She sits back down. She unfolds it first lengthwise and then crosswise again and again and again. It is pleated so heavily it curls in on her hand. The tiny scrawl is water-stained and full of crosshatches and arrows and seemingly intentionally illegible besides, but she knows what it says. She looks at it and then up again at Jessica's eyes.

"I was your only parent, the one who tucked notes in your lunches and talked you to sleep from bad dreams, and I also hurt you. I have a list here of the ways I did it if you'll let me read it."

Jessica nods.

Lynn looks down again at her paper and reads, pausing for a long while after each one to give it its due:

I let you clean up my vomit.

I passed out and let you worry I would never wake up.

I slapped your face when we argued.

I shoved you down the stairs.

She looks up at Jessica and sees the tears streaming down her face. "Is this all right? Should I keep going?"

Jessica nods again, firming her lips, her chin trembling.

Lynn looks down. The paper is quivering in her good hand, like a husk of something.

All your life I told you your father was dead to protect you from what he was.

Then, when you were sixteen, when I could see that the person he'd become in your mind was a better parent than I'd managed to be, I told you the truth and dared you to go see for yourself if you weren't better off with a mother who broke your arm by shoving you down the stairs.

She flips the paper over to see the last one on the other side:

And I failed to find you when you took me up on it.

"You were drunk, Mama."

"I chose to be."

Jessica wipes under her eyes with the sleeve of her sweatshirt. Then she takes a sip of her tea.

Lynn lays the paper on the table, curved and ribbed from years of folding and unfolding, and does the same.

They set their cups down but hold on to them.

The static on the baby monitor hisses.

Jessica says, "I'm sorry I left."

"You needed to."

"I'm sorry I went to him."

"Are you, though?"

"Of course." Jessica blinks. "I could have skipped it. All the grief he's caused me and my family."

Lynn shrugs. "Apparently not."

"What?"

"Apparently you couldn't just skip him. Me neither, by the way."

She stands and opens a drawer with a clatter. She takes out two teaspoons, and from the cupboard she gets a little saucer. She sets a spoon in front of Jessica and uses the other to pull the tea bag from her water and wrap the string around and around, squeezing it against the bowl of the spoon. Then she sets it on the little plate between them.

Jessica lets her tea keep steeping. She says, "But just think how much better life would be for both of us if we had."

Lynn shakes her head. "I don't know about that. If I'd skipped him, you wouldn't even be here."

She takes a sip, and Jessica watches her.

Lynn says, "Life is full of things that feel like traps. Our own weaknesses and mistakes. Unlucky accidents. The violence done to us by others. But they're not always what they seem. Sometimes later we see that they led us where we needed to go."

Jessica straightens. She shakes her head bitterly. "No—"

"I'm not saying they're not awful—"

"No way—"

"I'm saying they can be both. I'm saying it gets used."

Jessica gives her head another fierce little shake and then looks up at the ceiling and bites her lip to keep the tears from spilling over.

Lynn waits a second, watching her.

On the ceiling where she is looking there is nothing at all to see. Just plain white plaster and a bowl of frosted glass diffusing the light from a single bulb.

Lynn says, "That farm accident I lost this hand in? It was an accident he rigged for money, and I can't even say for sure that wasn't some kind of gift to me."

Jessica lowers her chin. An incredulous puff of air escapes her. "How do you figure that?"

"It made it just a hair too hard to drive a car when I was drunk. It's what forced me to ask those girls to board with me and help me out. Who knows? I might be dead if I had two hands."

Lynn looks at her over the top of her cup, elbows on the table, her good fingers and her bad holding her cup suspended. She shrugs. "Would anything be different for you if you'd skipped him? The kind of job you picked? The kind of husband you picked? The kind of mother you're turning out to be?"

She watches her daughter's face change, thinking about that.

Jessica presses a finger to the bowl of the spoon her mother gave her, tipping it up, and then lets it settle.

Lynn says, "Maybe you've got the whole mess with him to thank for some of what you love."

Jessica shakes her head again, looking down, crying finally.

Lynn says, "Maybe he's not our devil, but our angel instead. Or mirror. Maybe it's only ever ourselves we have to fight or forgive."

11

Facts

Vivian sits on a wooden bench in the hallway outside the courtroom. She leans forward a bit to open the purse she borrowed from Lynn, and we see that underneath her white cardigan sweater, the waist of her long dark blue skirt is pinned to cinch it small. She takes a tissue from a little packet and slips off a black vinyl pump to stuff it in the toe, where there is already a crumpled ball of white. Then she puts her shoe back on and sits up to snap the bag shut again.

She can hear footsteps on the stairs before she can see anyone—clicking steps she can tell are a woman's. She sees her face first coming up, soft brown hair cut short around a soft round face. The woman is wearing a white blouse and a tan skirt and black shoes, and the black briefcase she carries looks like a man's. She sees Vivian right away and starts smiling like she would meeting her at a bus stop—like she knows her and has been waiting a long time to meet her. She walks over and sits down beside her and puts her hand out over Vivian's lap to shake. She doesn't even check that she's right and ask Vivian's name. She just knows.

"Thank you for coming," she says.

Vivian shakes her hand, but she can't talk yet.

The woman says, "I know you didn't want to do this."

Vivian swallows hard.

The woman says, "That's common, you know. It makes a world of sense that you wouldn't want to be here. But I think you'll be surprised at how good you feel afterward. That's what most women report."

Vivian wraps the strap of her purse around her finger.

The woman looks at her watch, a white face rimmed in gold, with a black leather strap. She says, "The courtroom isn't going to be used for anything for another twenty minutes, but after that it will be busy all day. I think we should go in and check it out now while it's free, before you tell me your story."

Vivian gets the strap very tight, like a little spring coil, and then unwinds it.

Carla says, "I just think it's a good idea for it to be familiar to you during the trial. You don't want to be wondering and worrying. You don't want to feel surprised."

Vivian says, "Who told you about me? How did you know to come looking for me?"

"Your old neighbor, Mrs. Ainsley. And a few coworkers of your dad's, too, from the school."

She winds the strap again. "I didn't know so many people knew."

"They didn't know for sure. They might have helped you if they did. They just suspected. Then after you ran away—you were only fourteen, is that right?"

"Yes."

"After that they felt more certain."

Vivian swallows.

The woman leans toward her a little, resting her elbows on the knees of her smooth suit, like a mother. "So what I'd like to do first is show you the courtroom. So you can see where everyone is going to sit."

Vivian nods. "Okay."

She stands and collects her purse. She pulls down the back of her sweater over the bunched top of Lynn's skirt. Then she follows the woman through the double doors.

The jury box and witness stand and tables—everything inside is a honey-colored wood, and the floor is white linoleum. Their heels click as they walk down the aisle between the rows of benches, like church pews, that people can sit on to watch things be decided.

Carla says, "Do you see the witness stand there? I think you should try sitting in it if you would. To get used to it. I'll tell you everything while you sit there. So you can picture it."

Vivian walks toward it—a plain desk with a vinyl swivel chair behind, and another wood wall behind that. She has to take two steps up to sit. She looks down at the woman and all the empty seats and desks spread out below her.

The woman says, "I'll be standing here to ask you questions, and then behind that table there when your dad's attorney is asking you his own questions. This table is the defense table." She lays a hand on it. "So that's where the defense attorney will sit. And your dad will be next to him. When was the last time you saw him? Your dad?"

Vivian is rubbing a thumbnail along the edge of the desk. With her other hand she is holding the big purse in her lap. "Back when I left. When I was fourteen."

"You'll have to pass by him here when you come in. He'll be dressed in plain clothes. And he'll be sitting in that chair."

Vivian nods, looking not at the woman, but at the empty chair, picturing it. "Will he be able to talk? Will I hear him talk at all?"

"If he tries, he'll be stopped. You won't be in here when he sits in this witness box, and he's not supposed to speak from that chair. And the jury will be watching him—he knows that—so he's most likely to try to look unthreatening."

"But he'll be looking at me talking."

"Yes."

Vivian stops rubbing the table edge and holds Lynn's big purse again with both hands.

Carla says, "I want to tell you—you need to know his lawyer will try to seem nice, but the aim of his questions won't be nice. He'll be standing where I am, as close as I am to you, trying to make you seem like your memories aren't clear, but even if some are foggy you can just keep coming back to the ones that aren't. We can talk about that, and I can help you learn how to show the jury that no matter what he says about what you don't remember, there's plenty that you do. What you remember is enough."

Vivian's eyes are still on the chair.

The woman says, "He'll probably also try to make it seem like you might have a reason to make things up. He'll ask you about your life now, so next you and I should sit down in a room with some tea or hot chocolate for a few minutes and you can tell me as much as you can about what has happened to you since you left your dad's house. I can give you advice about how to describe it. But let me make this easy for you. No matter what you tell me, no matter what you've done since you left home, none of it can be the reason he did what he did to you, can it? You didn't cause it after you left, right? So we can just tell the truth, and I can tell you how to do that so the jury will not forget which thing happened first. That your dad chose to hurt you when you were just a little girl."

Vivian looks at her, finally, her big purse weighting her down in the chair. "You know what he used to say every time when he finished?"

"I surely don't."

Vivian's face screws up, staring at the empty chair. Her eyes fill. Then she says, " 'I know you'll never tell.' "

"Oh, honey."

She wipes her nose with her hand, her eyes still fixed on the chair where she knows now her father will sit and see her.

Later Vivian sits in a small room with a small conference table. A big plate glass window behind her shows the city laid out flat and glinting under the lowering sun—the normal parts and then the strip with the black pyramid, a castle with a roller coaster, and the big flat building of shiny gold that says MANDALAY BAY across the top. She has her back to all this. She is making small tears like battlements in the rim of a Styrofoam cup.

When Carla comes in, she looks up.

She has papers in her hand. "You're a very patient girl to wait for this. I wish I could have gotten them to you sooner, but I had a trial. I typed up all my notes. You can call and tell me if you think I got anything wrong."

The little white bits lay strewn around her elbows. "That's not why I wanted them."

"I didn't think so, but you still can if you notice things. I want you to."

Vivian puts the papers in Lynn's big purse. "Okay." She tidies the Styrofoam into a little pile and scoops it into her hand.

The woman reaches out a cupped palm, and Vivian looks at it a second and then dumps the bits into it carefully. The woman empties her hand into a waste can behind her, her blouse rippling in an invisible shaft of air from the vent above.

Vivian slings the bag strap over her shoulder. "Well . . ." She blinks and stands up. "I think I should get going now. If that's okay."

"Of course, Vivian. You were always free to go."

"I wanted these papers, though."

"I would too, if I were you. You've been brave. You've done something important already, and in a few weeks you're going to do more. You should be very proud of yourself."

"Can you tell me?—Where is he now?"

"He still lives in the same place. He's free until he comes here to court."

"Does he know he's going to see me?"

"Not yet. But he will. I'll have to tell his lawyer I spoke to you."

"Okay."

"I could imagine you might worry about that. I could imagine you might worry he'll try to contact you."

Vivian shrugs.

"Do you feel safe where you are?"

"Yes, ma'am."

"Because you're right that he could. It wouldn't be wise of him, but we can't keep him from trying."

"It's all right," Vivian says. "I'm ready, I mean."

In her little brown car, in the parking lot outside the big courthouse, Vivian locks the doors. The sun is sinking low in the sky, making something creamy orange of the clouds behind the palm trees along the center median. She slips the papers out of Lynn's big purse and holds them on the steering wheel:

PRE-TRIAL INTERVIEW WITH VIVIAN LOUISE ABLE

She scans through the Q and A lines until she reaches one on the second page:

Q: And I understand you have twin four-month-old babies?

A: Yes.

Q: Can you tell us about the father of those babies?

A: I don't know for certain who he is. When I ran away from my dad, I mostly paid for food by washing dishes at the Denny's on Tropicana. But I also got mixed up in prostitution.

Q: Mixed up?

A: A man told me I could stay with him. Then he wanted me to be his girlfriend. And then he said he needed my help doing a favor to some people he owed money to. It sort of snuck up on me what he was doing.

Q: And did you use birth control?

A: Yes. Condoms. But it didn't work this one time.

Q: Do you still work as a prostitute?

A: No. I quit so I could take good care of the babies.

On the road home she listens to music—something heartfelt and twangy again with a girl's voice and a lot of guitar. She has it turned up loud, and she has the transcript on the seat beside her. She looks at it at stoplights.

> Q: How old were you the first time he climbed in your
>   bed?
> A: Eleven.
> Q: The same year your mother died?
> A: Yes.

And at the drive-through when she gets a Frosty at Wendy's:

> Q: Did you ever ask him to stop?
> A: Yes.

And again when she pulls in at Copley's to fill the tank on her little brown car with the gas money Lynn gave her.

> Q: What did he say when you asked him to stop?
> A: He said if I hushed he could finish faster.

She sets the papers on the seat and gets out, pulling the sweater down over the bunched waist of Lynn's long skirt. The lot at Copley's is full like it was the night she first came here. She can see people leaning over their food at the tables in back. There are two trucks pulled in at the pumps, one of them a semi and the other a white pickup. Once she gets the nozzle in and sets the trigger, she takes a step back from the pump and reaches inside her car to pull the little zippered pouch with flowers out of Lynn's big purse. She sets it on the seat and removes a cigarette. She lights one up, her hands shaking, and takes a long drag, blowing smoke up toward the high ceiling of the shelter. There's a bird's nest up there, and she can see it. She watches to see if any birds peek their heads out while she smokes, listening to the rattling of the gas through the tube into her car.

Then she senses someone—a figure stepping around and standing on the other side of the nozzle to look at her—and she lowers her head to see.

It is the hunter.

"What's shakin'?" he says.

Vivian takes another drag.

He says, "I was about to grab lunch with my buddy. You want to join us?"

Vivian looks into the passenger seat of the white pickup and sees another man like the hunter, another middle-aged man looking down at her.

"No thanks," she says.

" 'No thanks,' eh?" He leans back against the side of Vivian's car, grinning.

Vivian doesn't say anything.

"Well, maybe I'll just wait a minute with you then," he says.

Vivian looks at the numbers speeding by on the tank dials. They always have such a frantic look. It's almost steadying for her somehow in a way she doesn't understand.

The hunter snorts. He looks over his shoulder at his friend in the truck. Then he makes his voice louder so his buddy can hear it: "Maybe I'll just wait so I can watch you pull out that hose when your tank is full."

"No, you won't," Vivian says.

"What?"

"No, you won't wait with me."

He snorts again. "Or what?"

Vivian taps her ash and then rests her other hand on the gas pump trigger. "Or maybe I'll pour gas on you and light you on fire."

He takes a step back.

Vivian keeps her hand steady on the pump nozzle.

"Crazy bitch," he says. He skirts around the front of her car toward his truck. "You better remember I know how to get to you."

"You do not," she says.

"Sure I do. Out at Lynn's place on Route 95."

There is a click, and the gas flow shuts off. Vivian takes the nozzle out and hangs it back on the pump. "That's where I live now, but you have no idea how to get to me."

12

Emotions

It is six p.m. and dusky, and Dana is sitting in the front seat of her Suburban watching the house. Through the window into the kitchen, she can see Jessica's mother handing her a baby. Then Lynn takes one up herself and they stand facing each other, talking, first Lynn, and then Jessica, and then Lynn again, and at the same moment, as if playing a mirror game, each of them reaches her free hand up absently to cup a tiny fine-hair-covered head.

Dana is hungry. She thinks she might finally be ready to eat.

The dogs bark when she gets out of her car and walks across the hard-baked lot toward the other Suburban. A circle of the low sun reflects off the dark driver's-side window and sets as Velasquez rolls it down.

"Why don't you go find a motel close by," he says. He smiles at her. "It's my night to sleep in a car."

"What if she doesn't decide to spend the night?"

"Then I'll call you and you can meet up with us."

"Okay. Can I get you anything? Dinner?"

"I'm good. I've got plenty in my cooler."

"All right." Dana nods. "Thanks," she says.

In the gray light along the state highway, the yellow neon sign on the roadhouse catches her eye from far away. COPLEY'S. There are plenty of cars in the lot, and it's crowded inside, but Dana is alone, so it is easy to find a single seat at the counter in back, where the waitress has to raise her voice over the sizzling from the big griddle behind her. Dana orders what she thinks her stomach can handle. French toast without syrup. And a plain baked potato. And ice water.

"If you say so," the woman says.

When she sets it down, Dana eats the French toast methodically, sipping the ice water between each bite, and then she lets the potato sit, watching the waitress fill coffee at all the tables until she can catch her eye and ask for a piece of aluminum foil and the check.

Dana drives along the road they traveled this morning. The potato wrapped in foil rolls on the seat beside her when she pulls into the lot of the motel next to the gas station. The Searchlight Inn, it is called. The lobby is just some metal office furniture in a room with brown curtains, and when she asks for a room, the old man behind the desk hands her a real key.

Dana's room is small, with a brown bedspread that matches the brown curtains and a threadbare industrial carpet the color of corn chips.

She sets her backpack on the bed and next to it her BlackBerry and the foil-wrapped potato. On the wall above the headboard is a small black-and-white picture of the motel in a black plastic frame, and the window overlooks the vast flat rock- and dirt- and weed-covered valley that stretches out to snowcapped mountains in the far, far distance. Dana stands there looking at that. She stands there a long time, not really moving, and then she turns and takes her cell phone off the bed. There is a chair in the corner—a narrow upholstered chair with wooden arms—and she sits down in it. She has to sit up unnaturally straight in it, but she doesn't seem to notice this, and she types a number into her cell phone, her face a calm nothing as it so often is, and listens to it ring. It only rings once.

"Dana! You'll never guess what happened after I left you that message this morning!"

"What?"

"Guess!"

"But you said I'll never guess."

"I know, but try!"

There is music in the background of his apartment. The Latin music again. She can hear his bird squawk. She can also hear water running.

"Are you cooking?" she says.

"I'm making rice. For rice pudding! I haven't tried that yet in my marathon of soft foods; isn't that a good idea? But wait! What's your guess?"

Dana looks around her room from her position in the straight-backed chair. At the brown-filtered light and the backpack and the shiny potato on the bed. She says, "You decided you don't love me."

"What?! No, crazy chica! What would make you guess something like that?"

"I was trying to think of something ironic."

"Wait, why would that be ironic?"

"Tell me what happened first."

"Okay—I got in a car accident!"

Dana blinks.

"I'm fine, I'm fine. But here's the amazing part."

"No injuries?"

"No, I'm fine, but get this—"

"Did you go to a doctor?"

"Yes, but get this—I was on my way to buy more Boost!"

"But I bought you Boost."

"I know, but I didn't know that yet. Darius and Leslie and Dino drove me to the wedding in their rental car so I hadn't been to the garage, and then on the way home it was four a.m. and we stopped at Denny's for pancakes; that's where I got the idea for rice pudding by the way, although theirs was plain and mine is going to have a flavor—piña colada!—and then on our way home from *that* we were driving along

La Cienega and I saw RiteAid and I said, 'Turn left! Turn left! I need Boost!' and he did, and we got hit by a Babies'R'Us truck."

"A Babies'R'Us truck."

"Yeah. He wasn't going very fast though, luckily."

"So everybody's okay?"

"Yeah. I spent the rest of the morning in the ER. They brought in an oncologist too just to make sure everything was all right with my treatment, but he said he didn't expect any adverse effects."

Dana stares at the shiny potato.

"Dana?"

"I'm here."

"Isn't that amazing?! We were just talking about that!"

"But you were talking about you *dying* in a car accident."

"True! So I'm glad it's not a total coincidence. Maybe somehow it was the fact that I didn't actually need the Boost that saved me. This pineapple smells funny; maybe I'll just make it coconut rice pudding. Okay, so what did you want to tell me?"

Dana looks again at the potato.

"Dana?"

She clears her throat. "I met someone from Aetna last night."

"Weird!"

"I did him a favor—before I knew he was from Aetna—and he gave me his card and asked me to think about what he could do to thank me."

"What kind of favor?"

"I delivered his wife's baby in the back of a car."

"Hot damn! Your job is nutty."

"It wasn't part of my job. I was on break, sort of. I was just—there."

"Have you ever delivered a baby before?"

"No, but it was part of EMT training."

"You're like a superhero. You're like Elastigirl. You need to get back in town so I can summon you."

"He's a senior claims examiner."

"Excellent. Life is excellent."

Dana smiles. "So you're always saying."

"Hey, do you think I cook the rice in cream, or add the cream after the rice is cooked?"

"I think you add it after."

"I wonder what would happen if I cooked it in cream too. Maybe it would be even creamier. Even better."

Dana smiles again.

He says, "So why would it be ironic if I'd decided I'd stopped loving you?"

"I've just been thinking about you a lot. I've been really missing you."

"Ha! More excellent. This sharing my superhero with the masses thing isn't all bad. I told you this trip might turn out to be good news for me."

"But you got in a car accident."

"Exactly. Good or bad, Grasshopper, you never know."

"Then I met the Aetna claims manager."

"Exactly! Warning: Jumbo load of shit may contain pony. For example"—there is a sound of metal striking metal in the background—"I think this cream is burning."

"I'm not sure you're supposed to boil cream."

"On the other hand, maybe it will just taste caramelized." Another clang. "Should I be watching those sexy Venetian blinds of yours for action anytime soon? You'll probably be back tomorrow, right? To your little Clark Kent lair?"

"We'll see."

"Ta-da! You're getting it."

She laughs. "We'll see."

Dana hears a shrill beeping in the background through the phone.

"Oh shit!" Ian says. "That's the smoke detector. I've got to go. Okay, mine will be the apartment with the charred curtains across the way. Bye!"

Dana continues listening a moment. Then she takes the phone from her ear and presses the red button and rests it on her pant leg, holding it there with one hand. She looks around the room, at the potato and the backpack. The room is so brown. The light is so dark and thick through the heavy curtains. The bed is bowed in the middle from the sleeps of people she will never know. And there are no sounds at all. There is a hushing noise from the passage of cars on the highway in the distance, but nothing individual, no evidence of coming or receding, just the white noise of it all.

Dana picks up the phone and calls him back.

The smoke detector is still wailing in the background, except louder now. Dana smiles.

"Hold on!" he says. "I still haven't got it."

"Can I just wait? Are you going to take the battery out?"

"That's why it's so loud. I'm on a chair right now trying to pry the top off."

She listens to it scream, and underneath that, a little rattling sound of metal against plastic. Then it stops.

"Phew!" he says. Then: "The best! I love that you called me back. You must really like me."

"There was something else I wanted to tell you before."

"What was it?"

"You were right about something else the night of your avocado party."

"What?"

"I didn't know it at the time or I would have told you. I only figured it out after I left, and then you were having your party and I thought I should wait and tell you alone, which I was going to do at the wedding, and then I got called for travel duty and I didn't want to text it so I had to wait for a break. . . ."

He laughs. "It can't be that bad. What is it?"

Dana clears her throat. "I was pregnant."

"What?! No way! That's fantastic!"

"No. I'm trying to say—I *was* pregnant. I bought a test at the drug-store after I left your apartment and tested positive. And then last night I went into the bathroom and my period had started, which means I miscarried."

"Oh. Well . . . shoot. Um . . . so you're probably happy about that, though, right?"

Dana looks around the bark-colored room, at all its dark, closed, straightened elements. The pillows are plumped and square, but there is that sag in the middle of the bed that reveals that people have slept there—many people, and for years and years. She looks at her legs in the too narrow chair. And her shoes aligned in the gold shag.

"I don't know."

"You don't know?"

"I don't know."

"Marry me!" he says.

She laughs, a kind of snorting explosion that also releases tears she reaches up to wipe immediately with the back of her hand. She is smiling again. "Shouldn't I try sleeping a night in your bed first?" she says.

"Is that a yes?"

She starts to cry.

"Dana?"

"I'm sorry."

"For what? Is that—are you crying?"

"Yes."

"Holy smokes!" There is some clear sympathy in his voice, but also a delight he can't repress. "What does it mean?"

"I just—" Her head tips back and she looks at the ceiling. It is covered in plaster with the texture of cottage cheese. She closes her eyes. "Uch. It's so awful."

"Try me."

"I feel so sorry for you."

"I *like* you, Dana. Remember? I like *you*."

"I can tell I need to think about this alone. Without you listening and waiting for my answer there. And it just seems so sad, for me even, but especially for you, that I'm a person who is better at *everything*—working, training, thinking, feeling, everything—alone. Isn't that tragic? Who wants to marry that? Isn't that your worst nightmare?"

"We'll see, sweet girl," he says gently, and he hangs up the phone.

Day 4

13

And So On

Lynn latches the gate on the little run next to the dog yard. Grace is lying on a pad there under the shelter, her stitches a long black line at her neck, and Sweetie Pie is lying in the dog yard with a little Jack Russell terrier who barks to let her know Lynn is passing.

Watching from the turnaround, Vivian has Emmaline asleep on her shoulder, her pink cheek flattened against the nap of her white sweater. Jessica is holding Sebastian, rocking him back and forth and saying, "Tell me something, sir." The empty baby carriers rest on the ground between them. When Vivian came home late last night, Lynn had already warned her by phone about the cars in the driveway, thinking they might scare her. She was waiting with tea, and she told Vivian that her babies were sleeping upstairs and that in the big bedroom below, her own daughter too was sleeping. That's all she'd said about her, and nothing more about the extra car, and because Vivian had traded enough with Lynn to feel safe now, she didn't ask. When she came into in the kitchen the next morning she had understood. Jessica was sitting alone at the kitchen table drinking coffee, and Vivian recognized her right away but pretended not to, just refilled her cup, because everyone deserves to feel known for the things they choose to offer up themselves.

It is almost noon now, and the three black Suburbans are lined up behind them. Lynn crosses back through the dog yard, a tangle of dogs around her legs, laughing and leaning to pat their heads and saying, "Come on now" when they cause her to stumble.

After she latches the gate behind her, she rinses her hands under a hose bib by the shed. Dana is there, picking up the tailgate mat from her Suburban, propped dry and clean now against the shed wall. The plastic Petco bag is looped over her wrist. She holds it open for Lynn.

"Can you use these?"

Lynn peers into the bag at the silver bowls and treats Dana used to care for Grace on her journey here.

"Sure." She wipes her hand and loops on the seat of her jeans. "Why don't you bring them here to my rescue assistant?" She leads Dana to Vivian and Jessica holding the babies in the center of her circle. "Have you met Vivian?"

"No, ma'am, I haven't," Dana says. And to Vivian: "I'm Dana— I won't try to shake your hand." Vivian still has a sleeping baby, and Dana herself has the Petco bag in one hand and her car mat in the other. "I just wanted to offer these extra bowls and treats. I'll lay them on the ground here." She sets the bag down. It rustles in a breeze almost too slight to feel and settles against Emmaline's empty car seat.

"Thank you," Vivian says.

Dana nods, still holding the car mat. No trace of Grace's blood remains.

Then, as if etiquette requires that they acknowledge their convergence, the four of them stand there a moment in silence, as if they might stay together; as if they are not about to continue on their separate paths. Because it is morning, the shadows their legs cast are long, fanning out like rays. The dogs know, though. They are barking like crazy. Dogs can always sense a departure.

It is Dana who gets them started, retreating without a word of parting to her Suburban.

Then Lynn clears her throat. "All right then."

"You ready?" Jessica says.

"Oh yes."

She turns to Vivian. "You'll be sure to call Ruth Ann if you need help?"

"I promise," Vivian says. "And I have your number too. But I'm going to be fine."

Lynn climbs up into the cab of her truck where a duffel bag sits on the passenger seat.

Jessica lays Sebastian in his carrier. "They're beautiful babies. Mom said you're a wonderful mother, and I can see that she's right."

"That's kind of you to say."

"It's the truth," she says, and she steps away and climbs into her Suburban. Both women wave at the girl and shut their doors.

Jessica pulls away first, then Lynn in her truck, then Dana behind her and Velasquez last, a procession of shiny black cars and Lynn's battered yellow one rumbling down the rutted drive toward the road that cuts through the red valley and disappears off near the pale white morning horizon.

Vivian picks up both carriers and goes inside. The bottles she made are sitting just misted in the pan of water on the stove, and this time she does not go to the couch to feed them. She takes them upstairs to Jessica's old room and settles herself on the daybed and feeds them there. The shades are drawn almost all the way down, like sleepy eyelids, and through the yellow fabric the sun tinges all the pinks in the room with a dim, thick, sunset-colored glow like the inside of a seashell. Vivian hums, and the babies suck so hard they both make that *squee* sound from time to time on the rubber of their bottles, until they are so full and relaxed that first he and then she falls asleep sucking, their mouths relaxing until the nipples fall aside, and little dribbles of milk go down their cheeks and into the collars of their sleepers. Vivian pulls her arms aside slowly, letting their weight settle onto the bed. They stir a little, Sebastian's arm flinching up quick and then falling slowly, slowly, as if through water, onto a little lace-trimmed tooth-fairy pillow with a pocket in front, and

Emmaline kicking, kicking, as if she is bicycling, before stretching her legs out, big toes tenting the feet of her yellow sleeper, and then going limp on Jessica's old bed.

Vivian scoots off now and leans to raise the rail Lynn had told her to look for. A little bronzed hook at each end swivels into an eye on the posts of the bed. There is a closet door in the room, and when Vivian opens it she sees that inside there is nothing on the hanging rod and nothing beneath, and this is where she sets the car seats, one next to the other, before she closes the door. Neither baby has stirred. They are both sleeping soundly on their backs in their new bed, and Vivian leaves the door open a crack and goes to her own room, where the liquor cartons full of her clothes lie at the foot of the bed. The dresser Lynn cleared is painted white, with little cut-glass knobs, and Vivian slides one open now and sees it lined with a pink shelf paper that curls a bit at the edges, and she sets about putting her own things away, emptying the boxes into the drawers.

On the road in her truck, Lynn twists the radio dials for music that matches her mood.

In her car, with her daughter's red shoes still beside her, Jessica does the same.

They do not stop, not when they pass Copley's, or the sign that says, NEXT GAS STATION 90 MILES. The desert around them greens and softens in small starts and gives way to grassed hills, the road cutting a way between, and each of them from time to time changes stations, not often finding the same songs but covering the same range of spirit—calls to courage, and reflections on sorrows past, and tunes of pure celebration—and after a long while, there is the ocean beyond as they wind down from a high spot toward the city below, highways snaking and all the land quilted gray, with jewel sparks of swimming pools and grassy yards and windows the sun catches, and the ocean in the far, far distance. Cars join them in increasing numbers, but they manage to stay in a line, Lynn sandwiched in, and like this finally they eddy off down a ramp onto a crowded boulevard banked with tall buildings and billboards. At stoplights, tourists cross, a few heads turning to wonder about the procession they make—three black Suburbans and a battered yellow pickup between, and they move along, the buildings crouching lower, restaurants now with umbrella tables and white-fronted stores with mannequins posing, and then slender, smooth-trunked palms with a languid bloom of leaves impossibly high above waving in the slight breeze. Then just houses finally—trim green lawns and hedges and high gates with a clean, clean sidewalkless street cutting between, and at last a pair of big gates opening, and Jessica pulls into the circle drive in front of her house, and her mother's truck rolls in behind her.

It is afternoon, the white stucco so bright that both women visor their eyes with their hands to see what is coming out the big front door: two girls running out and across the bricks to hug Jessica around either leg. They turn their heads to the side to assess the stranger beside her, and before they can speak a question, there is their father.

"Can I be the first one to hug you?" he says, and tears spring to the old lady's eyes. She lets herself be hugged, but stiffly at first, and then her arms go up to his back as if they remember what to do.

"Who is that, Daddy?"

"It's your grandma," he says, still gripping her tight. Finally he lets her go. "It's your Grandma Lynn."

The lady smooths the front of her sweater before she crouches down between them. Her boots are dusty. They even have whole pieces of mud dried on. And her soft cheeks are shiny with tears. "Hi there," she says.

"I thought you were dead," Jaya says.

"No she wasn't," says Prisha. "Remember? She just lived very very far away."

Lynn smiles. "Both things are kind of true."

"You were *dead*?" Jaya says.

"Only like a car battery can be."

"Oh, that kind."

Prisha looks at Jessica, whose cheeks are also shiny wet. "What happened to your hand?"

"A broken dog bit it," she says.

"Not a mean one?" says Jaya.

"No."

"And what about *your* hand?" Jaya says.

Lynn laughs. She wipes her eyes and smiles at her. "Same thing."

Behind the house, in the little cottage at the bottom of the pebble drive, Dana hands over the keys to the armored Suburban and walks back outside to get into her Jetta. She passes the avocado tree, and in this sharper light of midday, the tire swing reveals the cloaked figure with the pike to be lying on his back, afloat in two inches of rain water the sun never reaches, his red eyes regarding a firmament of worn black rubber bisected by the rope from which, to him, everything seems to hang. She stands him up in the water, looking out into the wider yard.

On the drive home, how is she different? She drives the speed limit, but we can see from how often she checks the speedometer that this is hard. And when she pulls up in front of the white horseshoe-shaped building, she parks not in the garage but out front, where she can see that his curtains—not charred but bright, colorful, ridiculous—are still flapping in his open window like flags. She gets out of the car and kicks the door closed, and she tries to walk, but no, she can't really do it. She laughs at herself, and Dana starts to run. She takes the stairs two at a time and hurries down the hall—a right turn, a right turn again, because already she can hear his music.

When she comes in the door, the room smells like citrus, and the counters are a-jumble with squeezed fruit and papers and that box of needles, and Dana sees that, well, yes, of course, Ian is sitting on the floor with both parrots on the Astroturf, feeding them peanuts he is shelling from the cow skull that spilled the spider plant from his window. She sets her backpack on the floor beside him, and the birds flap and fly up, up onto the couch cushions, while she herself sits down on top of him, in his lap, and he explodes with laughter. "Well, hello to you too," he says.

And she has to hug him, and that is when she says it, with her cheek pressed up against the ridge of scar on his neck, looking past him, over his shoulder, out his open windows.

"Yes," she says.

He pulls back to meet her eyes with his. "Yes?"

"Yes," Dana says, nodding, smiling, crying again just a little bit, thinking who is she all of a sudden? Where did she come from? Where did she go?

"Yes, I said. This is yes."

ACKNOWLEDGMENTS

Many people made it possible for me to complete this book through generous donations of time, expertise, and kindness. Some did it by patiently sharing technical information from their respective professional domains, understanding no doubt that I might get some of it wrong in spite of all their care. Others did it by reading (over and over) full drafts and excerpts of this story and sharing their honest impressions and thoughtful suggestions. A few shepherded it through the publishing process and played parts in making it into a beautiful book. I am grateful to all of them: Alexa Albert, Fred Appelbaum, David Byrd, Karen Karbach, Chip Kidd, TJ Klomp, Ellen Lackermann, Jordan Pavlin, Melanie Rehak, Becky Roe, Richard Shugerman, Chandler Tuttle, Amanda Urban, Jim Van Wyck, and Cassian Yee.

In the greatest number, people helped by encouraging and supporting me in an inspiring variety of less direct ways, and among these I count my siblings (the homegrown variety and those acquired in adulthood), my parents (again, of both types), my friends, and anyone who, in the years I was writing this book, was kind or helpful to me or to my children, a subgroup which is in itself heart-swellingly large.

ACKNOWLEDGMENTS

In a special category are Preston, George, Henry, and Emmy, who teach and rescue me daily with their love and ideas, and Jeff, who is ever my most devoted reader and friend.

A NOTE ABOUT THE AUTHOR

MacKenzie Bezos was born in northern California and studied creative writing at Princeton University. She received an American Book Award for her first novel, *The Testing of Luther Albright*. She lives in Seattle with her husband and four children.

A NOTE ON THE TYPE

The text of this book was set in Sabon, a typeface designed by Jan Tschichold (1902–1974), the well-known German typographer. Based loosely on the original designs by Claude Garamond (c. 1480–1561), Sabon is unique in that it was explicitly designed for hotmetal composition on both the Monotype and Linotype machines as well as for filmsetting. Designed in 1966 in Frankfurt, Sabon was named for the famous Lyons punch cutter Jacques Sabon, who is thought to have brought some of Garamond's matrices to Frankfurt.

Composed by North Market Street Graphics,
Lancaster, Pennsylvania

Printed and bound by Berryville Graphics,
Berryville, Virginia